Stay Very Close

ANGELA DRAKE

Heartline Books

Published by Heartline Books Limited in 2001

First published in the United Kingdom in 2001
by Heartline Books Limited.

Heartline Books Limited
PO Box 22598, London W8 7GB

Heartline Books Ltd. Reg No: 03986653

ISBN 1-903867-07-X

Styled by Oxford Designers & Illustrators

Printed and bound in Great Britain by
Cox & Wyman, Reading, Berkshire

ANGELA DRAKE

Angela Drake is a Chartered Psychologist who has worked in the education services, helping children with learning problems. She is the published author of several romances and mainstream novels and has also written for the young adult market. Her novels have garnered excellent reviews on both sides of the Atlantic.

In her spare-time the author enjoys reading, going to the cinema and listening to music. Angela lives in Yorkshire with her husband and other assorted pets!

chapter one

It was dark by the time Isabel got back from work. The windows in her basement flat in one of North London's pretty Victorian squares reflected the pale silver of a new moon as she walked down the stone steps leading to the entry door.

She turned her key and then paused before pushing the door open with her knee, easing herself and her laptop computer inside. As usual, a few scattered envelopes lay on the blue and orange mosaic tiles of the small vestibule. Isabel glanced at them, her heart accelerating slightly as she searched for a large brown envelope edged in black.

Don't let there be one, she prayed silently. Not tonight. I'm too tired and I simply can't deal with another problem. With a sigh of relief she registered that all the envelopes were small and white, not a single black edging in sight.

She sent up a prayer of thanks, pushed the door firmly closed and, before taking off her coat, hurried through the flat switching on lamps, pulling curtains and making the place look cosy and lived in.

There was a knocking sounding on the ceiling of her sitting-room. Three knocks, a silence, then three more knocks. Isabel smiled. It was her upstairs neighbour, Florence Proctor. She would have been listening for hours for Isabel to come home, anxious just to exchange a few words with another human being.

'Coming!' shouted Isabel, tilting her head and throwing her words upwards. She let herself out of her front door, ensuring that she closed it firmly behind her and that the latch had engaged. Florence was waiting at the doorway of her flat which comprised half of the ground floor of the tall, terraced house in which she and Isabel rented accommodation. 'Come in, come in, dear! Oh, I'm so glad to see you.'

'Are you all right, Florence?' Isabel asked, concerned at the strain showing in the older woman's face. Florence had never revealed her age, but Isabel guessed her to be well beyond seventy. This evening, her brow was deeply furrowed and there were fanned lines of anxiety around her eyes.

'Oh yes. Yes, of course,' Flo said brightly. 'I just thought you'd like a nice glass of sherry before you started cooking your supper.'

'Just a small one,' smiled Isabel, who found Florence's sweet, gluey sherry as appetising as drinking treacle.

Flo poured the deep-brown wine into cut glasses. 'Your very good health, my dear,' she said as she took the first sip. 'Have you had a busy day?'

'You could say that!' Isabel said ironically, recalling the frantic dashes from one meeting to the next, and the delicate negotiations with investment companies. The reassuring of worried clients.

'You work much too hard,' Florence said in a motherly way. 'And you're much too thin.'

Isabel gave a little smile. She recalled that when she had first come to live in her flat, decorating it in a minimal Japanese-inspired fashion, Florence had regarded her with suspicion. A tall, slender girl from Edinburgh with an aristocratic Scottish accent and a high-flying job as a financial consultant. And no sign of a husband!

But Isabel had called to introduce herself, and gradually Flo had warmed to her. Isabel might wear designer clothes and have the stylish, sensual allure of those girls who advertised exclusive fragrances on TV, but she always had time to help Flo when she needed a light-bulb changing or couldn't manage to get out to the shops because her arthritic knee was bad.

'What about your day, Flo?' Isabel enquired gently. 'You look tired.'

Flo drained her sherry glass and set it down carefully. She laced her fingers together and Isabel saw that her hands were trembling.

'They've been banging on my door again. Those children from across the road at number 29.'

'Oh dear! When did this happen?'

'This afternoon. They came about four o'clock, rattling the letter box and kicking the door.' She bit her lip and her eyes glittered with tears. 'And then again about half-an-hour later.'

Isabel reached out and took one of Flo's hands in hers. 'What did you do?'

'I just kept telling them to go away. I didn't open the door. I didn't dare, not even with the chain on. You see so many awful things on TV nowadays, don't you? Old people beaten up and…'

'Yes,' Isabel agreed. 'But I'm sure these children are just bored and making a nuisance of themselves. Not really dangerous.'

'Oh, I don't know about that,' Flo said. 'Sometimes I think I'm beginning to believe in evil. I never did before – I thought human nature was basically decent and good. But if you'd heard them shouting out. Such language! It makes me blush just to think about it.'

Isabel could imagine, and she felt a sharp surge of anger

on Flo's behalf. 'Shall I go and have a word with their parents and let them know what's going on?'

'Oh no!' exclaimed Flo. 'Oh, don't do that Isabel. The youngsters hate me already and they'd really have it in for me then.'

'Why should they hate you, Flo?'

'Because I'm old and doddery and feeble, that's why! On the scrap heap.' Flo stared angrily at Isabel as if she had asked a very stupid question. Which Isabel realised was the truth.

'I tell you what, Flo,' she decisively, 'I'll keep a lookout for those children at the weekend, and if I catch them at any mischief outside your door, I shall issue such dire threats they won't even dare set a foot across the road, ever again.'

Flo looked at her with a mixture of gratitude and deep scepticism. She squeezed Isabel's hand. 'If I'd ever had a daughter,' she said, 'I couldn't have wished for a better one than you.'

There were a few moments of companionable silence.

'Oh,' exclaimed Flo, looking guilty, 'I forgot to tell you, dear. One of those special delivery vans came today. I saw the man go down your steps with a little parcel, but I couldn't get down quick enough to tell him to leave it with me. I suppose they'll try again tomorrow. Were you expecting something? Something nice, hmm?'

Isabel's heart gave a little thud. A parcel? She was expecting no mail deliveries. So what could it be? Please God – not a follow-up to the hateful brown envelopes with their black borders and their disturbing contents.

'A surprise present from a young man maybe?' Flo suggested slyly. 'An admirer?' She looked hopefully at the young woman sitting opposite her, admiring her mass of gleaming russet hair, her candid hazel eyes and her smooth, creamy skin. It was high time Isabel had a good, steady man. One who would love and watch over her.

Isabel shook her head. There was no young man at the moment. She had given the last candidate for that post his marching orders a few months back, when she'd found him in a passionate clinch with a colleague's wife at an office party. Isabel was no prude, but she had firm views on loyalty, and she had not missed the man in question especially.

'Well, I expect they'll call again tomorrow,' Flo said reassuringly.

'Yes,' Isabel agreed, trying to shake off the unease that gripped her at the thought of the unexpected parcel.

She managed to banish the speculation from her mind whilst she listened patiently to the childhood reminiscences which invariably followed Flo's first sherry of the evening. But later on, cooking supper in her tiny immaculate kitchen, she found herself constantly returning to the subject. Who would send her a parcel through a special delivery service? She hadn't ordered any goods had she? Books from the Internet? Lingerie from the advertisements in the Sunday supplements? No, she couldn't think of anything she had requested in the past few weeks. So what could be in this package? What horrible, menacing, utterly-unwanted thing?

Stop it, she told herself, hating the way her thoughts were running on in such a haunted way. Of course, if it hadn't been for the seven black-rimmed envelopes and their disturbing contents, she would never have given a second thought to the arrival of a delivery service at her door. A parcel, she would have thought. Great. A lovely surprise.

In the morning she got up early and walked to the local shops, because she had invited an old school friend and her new husband to have supper with her that evening. Isabel loved cooking and when she got back to her flat, she pulled her purchases from the bags in satisfied anticipation of the preparations later on. She filled the fridge with ruby red tomatoes, fennel bulbs, baby lettuce, slabs of Parmesan and Scottish Cheddar, tubs of *crème fraiche*, fresh pasta and smoked salmon. She placed the French cheeses she had bought from the local delicatessen on a plain white plate and stored them in the cool stone pantry that was one of the original features of the house.

As she set the table which stood in the window of her sitting-room, she kept glancing out of the window, looking up towards the street, watchful for any sign of the neighbouring children who had been baiting Flo. And, of course, the arrival of a special delivery van.

All was calm and quiet for an hour or so, and she was in the kitchen whipping cream and eggs when she heard the door buzzer sound. Wiping her hands on a towel she walked to the door, conscious of a small drone of inner anxiety as she pulled the door open.

The man waiting outside was restlessly jingling a fat bunch of car keys. 'Taxi!' he said crisply.

Isabel frowned. 'I'm sorry?'

'Taxi. You ordered one for twelve noon.'

She shook her head. 'No.'

'Are you Miss Bruce? Of the Garden Flat, 22 Belsbury Road?'

'Yes.'

'Well then, you've a taxi ordered, Miss Bruce. To take you to Highgate Cemetery.'

Isabel stared at him in bewilderment and growing

concern. 'Highgate Cemetery! Why on earth would I want to go there?'

'Search me. Some people like to go and look at the old gravestones. Or meet a friend.' He raised his eyebrows suggestively.

'Well, I don't want to do either,' Isabel told him firmly. 'And I am absolutely, totally and utterly positive I didn't order a taxi to take me to Highgate Cemetery. Or anywhere else today for that matter.' She felt the colour flame in her cheeks as she spoke.

The man stared at her for a few moments. 'Fair enough. But if some trouble-making time-waster out there has it in for you, there's no need to take it out on me.' He trudged back up the steps with an exasperated sigh.

Isabel closed the door and leaned against it. A shiver ran down her back. Was there really someone 'out there' who had a grudge against her? Was the person who had ordered the taxi the same one who had been sending messages in black-rimmed envelopes? Was it time to call the police?

In the police station a mile down the road from Isabel's house, Detective Inspector Max Hawthorne was seated behind a computer trawling through a long index of criminals with a record of harassment and grievous bodily harm.

Jack Cheney, a constable on his team, stepped respectfully up to his senior officer. Hawthorne had only joined the North London team four weeks earlier, but his cool, enigmatic personality had warned every man and woman on the team to tread around him carefully. The Inspector had never been known to lose his temper or even to raise his voice, but his hooded, watchful grey eyes had the knack of making those around him feel they were blundering around blindfold in a minefield. Jack had the impression that Hawthorne was definitely not a man to cross.

Sensing Jack hovering behind him, Max Hawthorne spun round on his swivel chair. 'Anything from the house-to-house enquiries yet?'

'A few odds-and-ends of information, sir, but nothing of real interest.'

Max Hawthorne sighed. 'A young woman receives harassing mail and then gets brutally beaten up in a residential side street. No one knows anything, and no one has heard anything. Somewhat hard to believe, don't you think?'

Jack was not sure what to say, so he kept quiet.

'Any theories then Jack?' Max Hawthorne asked, making Jack's heart give a little warning thump.

Jack licked his lips. 'Well, sir, I'm all for backing the jealous boyfriend angle. After all, she *is* a very pretty girl.'

'Woman, Jack,' Max Hawthorne said coolly. 'As professionals we refer to females over eighteen as women. You wouldn't wish to be called a 'lad', would you? And you're – what, twenty-two, twenty-three...?'

'Yes, Sir. Twenty-three.'

'Right. You're a man, and the "pretty victim" is a woman. Don't forget.'

'No, sir.'

'And I think the jealous boyfriend is a promising avenue to go down, or maybe the jilted lover. Do we have anything on those possibilities?'

'Not yet, sir.'

'Well, let's work on it.' He swivelled back to the computer.

Jack was not sure whether or not he was dismissed.

'Is there anything good on TV tonight, Jack?' the Inspector enquired abruptly.

Jack was startled. Was it a trick question?

'Because if not,' said his boss, not waiting for an answer, 'We'll send a team out on the evening shift to make a start. There's nothing like entertaining people who are having a dull time at home on a Saturday evening, is there?'

'No sir,' Jack agreed, praying that his leave wouldn't be cancelled. He had a very hot date lined up and he wouldn't want to see it – her – slipping away. He held his breath. 'Will that be all, sir?'

'Yes. For now.'

Sensing that his boss had lost interest in him, Jack scuttled away.

Max Hawthorne sat very still and focussed, his eyes scrolling down the endless list of names. A young woman lay in hospital, her beauty wrecked by repeated blows from some brutally heavy blunt object. She was the second case of an innocent young woman subjected to mindless violence in the past ten days. He leaned back, surveying the shimmering screen – a little worm of dread slithering in his mind; some portent of wickedness, some awful premonition that the next beating would end in death. And then came that dreadful sense of powerlessness which would sweep over most police personnel from time-to-time. You could search and slog, but sometimes it was like looking for a needle in a haystack.

He closed the file and stood up, shrugging on his jacket. He knew that his team found him too abrasive, too dismissive of their simplistic theorising. He knew that he ought to make more effort to be sociable, go drinking with them in the pub, join in the crude jokes about sexual conquests.

But all he cared about now was the job. Bringing criminals to book, protecting the innocent. Vulnerable women, little children. Maybe when you'd tragically lost the only woman you ever loved, it was the only way to feel.

chapter two

After the disgruntled taxi driver had left, Isabel went back to the kitchen and got on with her preparations for supper that evening. Having checked that the pears she had been gently poaching in claret were now cooked, she turned off the heat and went back to whipping eggs and cream in preparation for the *crème brûlee* she would serve with them. She washed the salad vegetables she would serve with the pasta, dried them carefully and placed them in the coolness of the pantry, covered with a dampened white cloth.

The steady routine of food preparation was reassuring and soothing, so when the door buzzer sounded again it gave her a jolt, reminding her of the threat that seemed to be constantly hovering over her. She stood quite still biting on her lip. The buzzer repeated twice, more urgently, and her nerves thrilled with alarm. Cautiously she opened the door a crack and peered out.

'Parcel for you!' said a cheery-faced young man in a dark-blue courier uniform. He held out an innocent-looking package, wrapped in brown paper and secured with beige parcel tape.

Isabel stepped through the doorway and stared doubtfully at the package, finding it hard to reach out and grasp it.

The courier gave a friendly grin and it was clear that he was thinking she was the best thing he had seen all day. He jiggled the parcel playfully in his hand. 'Here, take it, my love,' he said, smiling at her hesitation, 'it won't bite!'

Isabel signed for the parcel and then turned it this way and that. 'It doesn't say anything about the sender.' She looked up at the courier. 'Do you have any record of who sent it, or which town it's from?'

He looked through the documents on his clipboard and said, 'No, sorry, I don't.'

'Oh.' Isabel bit her lip, staring doubtfully at the package.

'We don't always get sender details,' he said helpfully. 'And don't look so worried, it's too small to be a bomb.'

Isabel shook the package. There was a slight rattling noise inside. She frowned.

'I'll bet it's a lovely surprise,' the courier said, in encouraging tones. 'One of those you'd never guess until you've opened it up. A present from a boyfriend perhaps?'

'No,' Isabel told him firmly, giving the parcel a further tentative shake and pulling at the fastening.

The courier now seemed as curious as she was. 'Here,' he said, taking out a pair of folding scissors, 'you never know what to expect these days. Maybe it's not a good idea to take it in the house. Why don't you open it up right away?'

'I think I will.' Isabel carefully cut the tape and tore away the brown wrapping paper. Inside, there was a cardboard box within which was a nest of tissue. There was no letter, no card. Her mouth drying, Isabel parted the tissue. She found just one object inside. It was a hypodermic needle, the kind used by doctors for injecting drugs. The tip glinted in the light, sharp and bright with menace. She let out a groan of shocked amazement then tore the tissue from the box, searching beneath it for some clue as to the sender's identity.

There was nothing. Glancing again at the courier, she saw that he was shaking his head in disbelief.

'What kind of deranged person would send me this?' she exclaimed, trying to think of any likely candidates who would find it entertaining to send such a horrible anonymous gift.

Since the envelopes had been arriving, she had been over and over this ground, but she could think of no one. Obviously, as a manager, she had had to make some tough staffing decisions, and there were one or two people passed over for promotion or moved to another section who might consider themselves her enemy. There were also one or two difficult clients who might believe she had failed them when the investments she had recommended hadn't satisfied their greed. But she could think of no one who would use such a cruel, underhand way of showing a grudge.

She replaced the needle in its bed of tissue paper and began to cover it up.

'I'd chuck it away if I were you,' the courier said bluntly. 'Get rid of it! Forget all about it.'

'That was my first thought,' she told him. 'But maybe there's some clue somewhere in this package about who sent it. If I throw it in the bin, I'll lose any chance of finding out.'

'Yes, I see your point.' He chewed his finger for a moment. 'Listen, perhaps I could do a bit of digging when I get back to the depot. Maybe find out which of our branches the package came from. Ask around. Someone might know something.'

'That's really kind,' Isabel said with a grateful smile.

He winked. 'Nothing's too much trouble for a nice lady like you.' He sprang up the steps and swung himself into the bright-yellow van parked beside the railings.

Isabel shut and locked the door. She spent a few moments thinking and then knew that things had gone beyond merely trying to sort them through in her head. She had been receiving regular hate mail for the past four weeks. Now someone wanted her to jump in a taxi and go off to cemetery, and just to hammer the point home he – or – she, although she didn't for one moment really believe it was a 'she', had sent her a reminder of how easy it was to kill someone. She imagined herself captive and helpless, a few milligrams of a lethal drug injected into one of her main veins. The cemetery would be the next stop!

It no longer mattered that she was a strong, independent woman with a responsible job. A woman who dealt with clever and devious people as a matter of routine – and was not often put down. It didn't matter that by involving other people in this growing nightmare, she would inevitably be admitting weakness, vulnerability and fear. What was happening to her could escalate into a matter of life and death. And she would very much prefer to stay alive.

The female officer she was put through to at the local police station was friendly and impersonal. She took Isabel's name and address and asked her to describe just what had happened to make her worried. Isabel thought the woman's reaction to the two most recent events was decidedly low-key.

'Has anyone tried to stop you in the street, or to enter your premises?' she asked, as though reading from an auto-cue.

'No.'

'Have you any idea who might be harassing you? An

ex-boyfriend perhaps? That is the most usual explanation.'

'No!' said Isabel, her voice shaking with frustration. 'I have no boyfriend at present and I split up perfectly amicably with the two I've had in the past. And neither of them could ever have stooped so low as to...to be so evil!' She knew this was exactly the wrong thing to say as soon as she'd said it. Too emotional, too melodramatic. Typical reaction of a hysterical woman. And wasn't everyone supposed to have some potential for evil? Cold shivers of fear trickled down her spine.

'All right, madam,' the operator said soothingly. 'We are rather busy at the moment, but we will get someone round to see you as soon as we can. In the meantime, we would advise you to keep your doors and windows secure and to be extra vigilant when you're walking out alone.' She sounded as though she were reciting a well-rehearsed speech.

Isabel found her hands wobbling as she put down the phone. She flew to the door and checked that the latch was secure. All of her windows were closed, as the autumn was drawing to a close and winter coming on, leaving a damp chill in the air. But still she felt the need to check that they were firmly shut. From the corner of her eye, she saw three children of around ten to twelve years old cross the road and dart up the steps leading to Flo's flat.

Seized with uncharacteristic fury, she flung herself out of the front door and raced after them. They were huddled around Flo's letter box, sniggering and nudging as they pushed open the flap and mouthed abuse, calling Flo an old bag, an old hag who had lost her marbles, and daring her to come out and catch them if she could.

'*What* do you think you're doing?' Isabel called out

with a low throbbing menace that brought them spinning round to face her, their faces wide-eyed with the shock of discovery.

'Nothing,' said the taller of the two boys, his eyes opening in a show of innocence. 'Honest.'

'I'll tell you what you're doing,' said Isabel, her eyes like ice. 'You're making an innocent woman who lives on her own feel very lonely and afraid. Had you thought about that?' The two younger children, one a girl, the other a curly-haired boy who could be no more than seven or eight now Isabel saw him up close, looked doubtful and shame-faced.

The taller boy straightened up, the lines of his face set hard and stony. 'So what are you going to do about it?' he challenged Isabel.

'I shall inform the police,' she said softly.

Dismay crumpled the boy's face. He looked around him, judging the chances of a quick escape down the steps. But Isabel was blocking the way, and looking extremely formidable.

'Nah!' he scoffed, but she could see he was rattled. 'You're just putting the frighteners on us.'

'No, you're quite wrong. I had to call the police earlier on another matter. They could be here any minute. And when they do come, I shall tell them where you live and about the way you've been persecuting Mrs Proctor. I know quite a lot about you all.'

All three suddenly looked terrified. They stood transfixed, staring at her, believing her, full of horror at the power she was threatening to use. Isabel did not know whether their fear was of the force of law – which she doubted would be very formidable, given the circumstances – or of the anger of their parents. She did not particularly care. Her main concern was to get them off Flo's back.

'OK. I'll give you one last chance. If you promise never to come up these steps again or do anything at all to upset Mrs Proctor, then I promise to say nothing to the police. But if I see or hear so much as a whisper from you that I don't like, I shall send them round to ask some very awkward questions. Do you understand?'

They nodded. 'You must promise. Each of you must say that you promise me,' she insisted.

When they had each made their solemn and subdued recitation, Isabel nodded in acknowledgement. 'Now vanish,' she hissed at them, making her eyes sinister with threat, 'before I change my mind.'

They scooted away like squirrels pursued by an angry dog.

Isabel went in to Flo's flat and sat with her for a while, explaining what had happened, reassuring her that she considered the children basically harmless, and that she would be vigilant in ensuring that they didn't bother Flo again.

When she got back to her own home, she felt her usual well-being begin to trickle back. Taking positive action in the face of bullying had energised her, given her a sense of regaining control over what happened in her life. The letters, the unordered taxi, and the hateful unwanted gift had made her feel as though she were a puppet being operated by some unknown controller who was pulling at her strings, manipulating her emotions and sending them off in whatever direction he wished. Even when she was quite a young child, Isabel had always resisted dancing to someone else's tune. She had not been rebellious or defiant, but had always found a way to be true to herself.

Now, however, she was beginning to understand that it would not be hard for a determined ill-wisher to steal her quiet inner strength away, to turn her into the kind of person who jumped nervously every time something slightly unusual happened.

But she was not going to let it happen. No, she told herself, glad to have faced up to the worst at last, that most certainly wouldn't happen. I'm one of life's lucky people. I'm strong, I'm healthy, and I have the courage to accept and combat life's difficulties as well as grasping all the good things. I've had a secure, happy childhood and wonderfully loving parents. All the things that allow a person to develop the determination to deal with whatever life throws at them.

When she welcomed her guests later that evening, her steel-coloured velvet dress clinging to her figure, her hair freshly washed and left loose around her shoulders, there was no trace of anxiety on her face or in her manner. In fact, Suzie, her one time school friend from her Edinburgh days, told her she was looking quite 'fabulous'.

Isabel was introduced to Suzie's new husband, Robbie, and the evening moved along on oiled wheels as the newly-weds chatted enthusiastically about their fairy-tale wedding, their fantastic honeymoon in the Caribbean and their wonderful presents which fitted so perfectly into their trendy, new house.

Isabel listened politely as a good hostess should. She realised that Suzie had moved into a different world now that she was married. She knew too that her old friend regarded her, Isabel, with barely disguised pity because she didn't have a steady man.

As the evening wore on, she found that she was no longer listening to Suzie's gush of information. She found herself glancing at the curtains, wondering if she could see a figure standing beside the window. Someone watching. Waiting. Counting out the minutes until the guests left and Isabel was alone to face the long hours of darkness. The sense of menace she had so bravely pushed away came creeping back, winding tentacles of fear around her like swirls of fog beyond which dark shadows lurked.

She had just finished pouring coffee and offered Robbie malt whisky when the door buzzer sounded. Three times, loud and urgent.

Isabel tensed, her body stilling into poised alertness like an animal scenting the wind.

Her guests looked at her enquiringly.

'Shall I get it?' Robbie asked courteously.

'No, no. I'll go.' Isabel jumped up, not wanting either of them to guess at the shocking state of her nerves.

She secured the chain carefully across the door opening, making a note to purchase a stronger one as soon as possible. 'Who is it?' she called through with as much calm authority as she could muster.

Peering through the narrow opening she saw two men stood outside, looming out of the darkness, silhouetted against the light from the lamp in the street directly above.

'Police, madam,' said the taller man, showing an identification badge. 'Might we come in and to speak to you, please?'

chapter three

Isabel's heart slowed a little from its panicky racing. 'How do I know that badge isn't a fake?' she asked.

'You don't, madam. Why don't you ring the local station and ask them to verify the existence of Inspector Max Hawthorne and Constable Jack Cheney?' The voice was low and measured, full of indisputable authority.

'No, I believe you,' she said, after a pause.

'Then might we come in?' the tall man asked with a touch of impatience.

'You want to talk to me *now*?' she exclaimed.

'Yes.'

'It's past midnight.'

'We saw that your lights were still on. And you did request a visit. Quite forcibly, I believe.' The impatience was growing.

Isabel had the sense that it wouldn't do her any good to argue with this man. She slid back the chain and opened the door.

The two men seemed to fill her hallway. She showed them through into her sitting-room where Suzie and Robbie were still sitting at the table, their faces startled and curious.

The inspector nodded to them and murmured a perfunctory, 'Good evening.' He turned to Isabel, 'I think what we have to talk about is confidential, madam.'

Isabel stared at him, angry that he expected her to quickly despatch her guests. As she watched him, it struck her that he was exceptionally good-looking in a wild, eagle-like way, and it surprised her that she should register the faintest interest in his attraction at such a time. 'You're suggesting I should ask my guests to leave?' she said, matching his cool manner.

'Yes.' No explanation, no apology.

Isabel was angry at his arrogance, but she felt a surge of hope as she contemplated his stern features. From raw instinct, she understood that if anyone could help her to stop the nightmare that had begun for her, this man could. The force of his will, his steely determination and his potential for making things move and shake seemed to shimmer in the air around him.

'Darling, we're already on our way,' Suzie said breathlessly. 'Don't worry, we'll see ourselves out.'

'You most certainly won't,' Isabel told her, striding through into the hall and plucking their coats from the banister rail.

'Will you be all right?' Robbie asked her anxiously as he helped Suzie into her coat.

'Yes, fine. I'll tell you about it later.'

'Izzie, darling – it's not anything tragic is it? Them calling at this time. Not a death or…' Suzie was at last lost for words.

'No, mothing like that. I was expecting a visit – although not so soon. Or should I say so late?' She gave a wry smile.

'He's rather dishy, the tall commanding boss-man,' Suzie whispered, her eyes opening wide in a gesture of appreciation.

'Hmm,' said Isabel. She kissed them both, opened the door and watched until they had reached the road and were walking towards their car. Returning to her sitting-room, she found the younger officer standing uneasily in the middle of the floor. He looked both nervous and fed up, Isabel thought. Which was probably entirely understandable when you reflected he was working after midnight on a Sunday morning, and with a senior colleague who looked as friendly as a box of sharp knives.

The inspector was prowling around her room, peering at photographs, examining the Chinese vase that had once belonged to her mother.

'It's a Georgian replica of an old Chinese design,' Isabel told him helpfully. 'One of a pair. The other got broken, which is a shame because a matching pair is four times as valuable as one on its own.'

The inspector swivelled round to face her, his gaze steady and penetrating. Isabel gazed back. There was something mysterious about him, she decided. His face was that of a warrior, like those she had seen on overseas trips, carved into the stone of ancient palaces. His hair fitted that scenario, thick and black, not curly but not wavy or dead straight either. But his skin was pale and his eyes silvery grey, like a stormy sea. Maybe he had an Arabian knight in his distant ancestry?

'May we sit down?' he asked, polite yet coolly distant. Isabel made a gesture of invitation and the constable sat on one of her ornate Edwardian ebony chairs. He looked as though the handle of a sweeping brush had been pushed down his back. The hawk-like Inspector, in contrast, settled in one corner of the soft, squashy leather sofa and looked as gracefully relaxed as a big jungle cat. And just as vigilant.

Isabel perched in the opposite corner of the sofa. She did not feel at all relaxed.

'May we have your full name please, madam?' the

inspector requested. He flicked a glance at his Constable who hurriedly took out a notebook and a pencil. Obviously the junior man was to act as scribe, leaving the lofty inspector free to keep his informant under the closest surveillance. At least that was how Isabel summed up the situation.

She cleared her throat. 'Isabel Violet Fortescue Bruce.' There were occasions when she wished her parents had not been so extravagant in their bestowing of names. She watched the constable struggle to get them all down. 'Fortescue was my mother's family name,' she explained.

'And your friends call you Izzie,' the inspector observed.

'Some of them.' She realised he must have picked up the hushed conversation in the hall as Suzie and Robbie were leaving. She wondered if he had heard Suzie's assessment of his male attractions, and guessed he had heard everything. Prickles of warmth crept up the back of her neck.

'Your date of birth, please.' He had not taken his eyes off her since he sat sat down.

She gave it, watching the inspector silently calculate that she was coming up to twenty-eight-years old. His subordinate continued to scribble.

'Are you married?' he asked.

'No.'

'Have you ever been married?'

'No. And if you want to know my occupation, I'm a financial consultant.'

He was silent for a few moments, as though thinking through the information she had given him. 'When you telephoned the station earlier on, you indicated that you had been on the receiving end of some harassment? Is that correct?'

'Yes.'

'A taxi you had not booked called to take you to Highgate Cemetery? And then you took delivery of a packet from an unknown sender and it contained a hypodermic needle?'

'Yes, that's correct.'

'Did you make a note of which taxi service called?'

'No,' Isabel admitted, realising the stupidity of her omission.

'Or the driver's name or number of the cab?'

She shook her head. 'I wasn't thinking clearly. I was shocked. Wouldn't you be unnerved if a taxi arrived to take you to a cemetery?'

He shrugged. 'Maybe you have some interest or family connections regarding Highgate Cemetery.'

'No, none at all,' she said sharply. 'My family are from Edinburgh and the Scottish highlands. The ones who are dead are all buried in Scotland. I'm a relative newcomer to London. I've only been here for two years.'

The constable was writing furiously now, but Isabel judged that his labours were largely unnecessary. She was sure Inspector Hawthorne would recall every word she said with complete accuracy.

'Did you come to London as a result of a job offer, or for personal reasons?'

'For the job. I joined a team of ten consultants with a large insurance brokers. Three months ago, I was appointed manager of the department.' The boasting made her wince, she was usually rather reticent about her career success. She realised that she had a strong need to let the inspector know of her achievements, to prove herself in his eyes. How odd!

'Do you have a "partner", Miss Bruce, or an intimate relationship of any kind?' he asked levelly.

Isabel felt her nerves give a jolt. It was as though she were being asked to undress in front of this inscrutable man. 'Not at present,' she said stiffly.

'And in the past?'

'A couple of relationships.'

'But no one now?' he insisted.

'No.'

'Are you sure? No boyfriend – however casual?'

'No boyfriend,' she said wearily, wondering how many people she had assured on that point in the past twenty-four hours.

'No special friend, then? Either male or female?' One dark eyebrow raised slightly. She noticed that he had very beautiful brow bones, high and arched.

'Are you trying to ask if I prefer women to men?' Isabel asked coldly, conscious of the constable shifting uncomfortably in his chair.

'Very well then, *do* you have a girlfriend, Miss Bruce?'

'No, Inspector Hawthorne. Do you?' she responded as quick as a flash.

He gave her a long steady look. 'No, Miss Bruce, I don't. I have to ask these questions, you appreciate,' he said calmly.

'I think you should concentrate on the harassment I've reported,' she told him.

'Yes, indeed.' He turned to his colleague. 'Perhaps you have some questions you would like to ask Miss Bruce?'

The constable jerked into a new alertness, his already pink cheeks deepening to magenta. He cleared his throat noisily. 'Well, Miss Bruce, could you tell us some more about the packet you received?'

'I can show you it,' she said, getting up and retrieving it from the bottom of the small cupboard in the hall where she kept her vacuum cleaner. She offered it to the constable who turned it over in his hands, just as she had done earlier. She noticed that his hands were shaking slightly, probably as a result of his boss watching him like a hawk tracking a mouse.

'Wait!' Inspector Hawthorne interposed as the constable lifted the lid of the box. 'Miss Bruce, did you touch the needle? Did you handle it?'

Her heart sank. Yes, of course she had. And, of course, she would have left her fingerprints all over it, probably obliterating any other ones. The forensic people would have no joy with it. She had watched enough TV dramas to know that. 'I wanted to see if there was any message in the packet, any clue as to who had sent it.'

Inspector Hawthorne declined to comment, but he took a surgical glove from his pocket and handed it to the younger man who hastily pulled it on. 'Have a look, Cheney. See what you can find.' He turned back to Isabel. 'What were your thoughts when you received this packet, when you saw the contents?'

'Shock. A sick feeling. For me, hypodermics are associated with drug injections. Two years ago I took my retriever dog to the vet to have her put down when she was fourteen. The vet filled the syringe and put it in a vein in her leg. Her heart stopped in a few seconds and she was gone.'

'So you see this gift as a death threat?'

She let out a gasp of dismay. 'That was too near the bone. Brutal and cruel,' she accused him.

'Yes. But we need to examine every aspect of this case, don't we?'

She bowed her head. She felt exhausted and she wanted the inspector and his sidekick to go away. To leave her in peace so she could sleep and forget this whole horrible business. But, at the same time, she recalled her fear of being alone through the night.

'And you can think of no one who would send you such a present?' the inspector continued.

'No. It's an unnatural act. Sick. I don't know anyone like that.'

The inspector gave an impartial nod. 'So your family live in Scotland?'

Isabel blinked at his change of tack. 'My mother died when I was ten. My father lives in Edinburgh. He's in his seventies now and rather frail, so I try to see him every couple of months or so.'

'I see,' he said. He was watching her very carefully, but his face revealed nothing of what was going through his mind, or his judgement of her. 'And are you an only child, Miss Bruce?'

'Not quite. I have a half-sister, Luisa, who was the child of my father's first marriage. He was divorced before he married my mother.'

'I see. And where does your sister live?'

'Out of suitcases mainly. She has a little flat in London but she's in Australia at the moment, visiting her mother.'

He nodded slowly. Silent, deliberating.

'Is all this quizzing about my family relevant?' Isabel asked.

'It could be.'

'I don't think so,' she said coldly.

'Do you think the two unpleasant events of today could

be a joke?' he asked. 'A sick joke, but nevertheless, not meant to be taken seriously?'

'No!' she protested, 'Absolutely not.'

'But why do you say that when you can think of no one who would do such a thing?'

'I just know,' she said stubbornly. 'Call it woman's instinct if you like. I simply know!' She heard the pitch of her voice rise, a touch of hysteria about to break out and she checked herself. There was a long silence, then the constable glanced furtively at his watch.

'Is there anything else? Anything you haven't told us?' Max Hawthorne asked softly.

She felt her palms dampen with moisture, her breathing accelerate. 'I've been getting hate mail,' she said.

Both his eyebrows went up this time. 'Why didn't you tell me this before?'

Isabel looked down and brushed an invisible crumb from the skirt of her dress. 'Because I find it very difficult even to think about it. They were horrible letters, disgusting, shaming.' Her face burned as she recalled the cheap, lined notepaper tightly folded inside the black-framed envelopes. And then the intimate insinuations revealed as she unfolded the paper, the dirty whispering quality of the messages.

'And may I see these letters?'

'No,' she said, feeling once again shown up as thoughtless, maybe even stupid. 'I took them to the office and put them in the shredder.'

'Oh dear,' he said mildly. He pondered for a few more moments and then stood up. The other officer immediately sprang to his feet, as though jerked by strings.

Isabel remained firmly seated. 'Don't you want to know more about the letters?' she demanded.

'Not tonight, Miss Bruce. I think we've gone as far as we can for now.'

'Surely you can't ignore such an important piece of evidence.'

'But there is no evidence,' Max Hawthorne pointed out.

'You have my word for it,' she said. She stood up and faced him squarely. 'Do you think I'm a liar?'

'I don't know you well enough to say at this stage, Miss Bruce.' He picked up the packet which the constable had placed on a side table. 'We'd like to take this with us. Constable Cheney will give you a receipt and we'll return it as soon as possible.'

'You can throw it to the bottom of the Thames as far as I'm concerned,' Isabel said heatedly. 'I never want to see it again.'

Again the inspector gave no visible emotional reaction. But at the door, he turned to Isabel and surprised her by offering his hand. She took it, finding it firm and warm. She had an urge to pull him back into the flat and keep him close by to protect her. He was not a man to offer comfort. She did not like him, but she had a sure knowledge he was a man she could trust not to let any harm come to her.

'You think I've been wasting your time, don't you?' she asked him, still holding his hand.

'No, I don't think that, Miss Bruce. I'm going to get the forensic team to give us a report on the package and, after that, we can have another talk.'

'Do you think I'm making a mountain out of a mole-hill?' she asked, drawing her hand from his.

'I'm quite sure you're not. Do please feel free to call the station any time if you have concerns before we speak again. And in the meantime, be very careful about your house security. And take the usual precautions when you're out walking by yourself. Dark, lonely places are best avoided.' A routine recitation, very assured and correct…and stripped of any emotion.

Isabel closed the door, drew the chain across and returned to the sitting-room. She stood for a few moments, her hand resting on the corner of the sofa where Max Hawthorne had been sitting. After a while, she moved to the table and slowly, methodically began to stack up the dirty plates and dishes before carrying them carefully through to the kitchen.

'So what have we learned about Miss Bruce?' Max Hawthorne asked Jack Cheney as they drove away from Isabel's flat.

Jack paused. 'I thought she was very…genuine,' he said cautiously.

'You thought she was telling the truth? About the taxi, about the letters?'

'Well, Sir, it's hard to say.'

Max laughed. 'Come on Jack, tell me what you really think, not what you think I want you to say.'

Jack made a hurrumphing noise.

'You thought she was a real looker didn't you? And intelligent and sparky and sexy. Yes?'

'Well, yes. But I didn't think that was, well, relevant to the case, sir.'

'Of course it's relevant,' Max said impatiently. 'In the case of targeted victims, the personality of the victim is often the key. What does the pursuer see in her? What signals is she giving off that make him want to frighten her to death?'

'Mmm,' Jack agreed doubtfully. 'But shouldn't we be thinking more about the pursuer – the criminal?'

'But what have we got to go on so far? We know virtually nothing about him. At the moment, all we've got to work with is Isabel Bruce and her magnetism for him. The only important thing we know about him is that he's interested in her, or women like her.' He realised that Jack Cheney hadn't much clue what he was driving at. Jack would have expected him to ask far more questions about the hypodermic and the taxi and the letters. Simple questions based on facts and the here and now. But all that would come in time. A first interview was mainly to chart the territory, find out where it would be useful to dig in the future.

'Are you sure it's a "him", sir? Maybe it's a woman,' Jack suggested.

'No,' said Max, 'It's a man, I'm sure of it.'

'So what did *you* think of her, sir?' Jack asked, suddenly cheered and emboldened as he realised his boss was driving him to his home and not back to the station.

'All those things you thought. And also that she is very much a woman on her own. Her mother's dead, her father's an old man who lives miles away. And she has no close family except a half-sister. No boyfriend.' She's lonely, he thought, his sympathies aroused. He pictured his empty soulless flat near Tower Bridge. It takes one to know one, he decided with a grim smile.

'Do you think she ties in with our search for "The Batterer", sir?'

'I did think that was a possiblity when we got the information from her call. She's a professional young woman like the other two who were attacked. Living in the same district.'

'And very tasty,' Jack broke. 'Sorry, attractive,' he corrected himself hastily.

'Quite. But the others didn't get hate mail. Just a lock of their own hair.'

'Creepy,' said Jack. 'Do you think she's in danger?'

'I'm not sure at this stage,' Max said carefully, although privately he was worried. The notion of this beautiful young woman being the target of some twisted and dangerous criminal made the breath stand still in his chest.

'Shouldn't we organise some protection for her?'

'I can't see our Chief Super authorising manpower on the evidence we've got so far. Can you?'

'No,' Jack agreed.

Max brought the car to a halt outside Jack's 1930's semi-detached house. 'Goodnight,' he said. 'And thanks for your help, Jack.'

Jack got out of the car. He glowed at the simple words of appreciation. Hawthorne might be moody and have weird ideas on detection methods, but he knew how to inspire loyalty.

As Jack let himself into his house, Max turned the car round at the end of the street and drove straight back to Isabel's street in North London. He found a space to park the car at a short distance from her flat where he could see the steps and her doorway. Letting the window down a couple of inches. he settled to keep a watch until it grew light.

Isabel loaded the dishwasher, then washed the silver cutlery and crystal glassware that had belonged to her parents by hand in warm soapy water. She tidied the sitting-room, plumping up cushions, picking crumbs from the polished wood floor, making sure the flower arrangement of stargazer lilies had sufficient water. Anything to avoid going to her bedroom and staring sleepless into the dark.

It was after two-thirty in the morning when she fell into bed. The events of the day had exhausted her and when she lay down she was very soon mercifully drowsy. She waited for the lines from the hate letters to replay in her head as they had done for the past few nights. But as she drifted into sleep, it was not the evil letters or the ghastly hypodermic that claimed her thoughts. What stayed with her was the last image of the day; that of Inspector Max Hawthorne's face. It stole silently into her mind and crept into her dreams so that she slept safe and peaceful until the morning.

chapter four

A week passed and there were no more unwanted 'gifts', and no more disturbing letters. Her working life proceeded in its usual way and on her evening visits to Flo it appeared that the bullying children had taken Isabel's warnings to heart. That was cheering and Isabel began to hope that whoever had taken a sadistic interest in taunting *her* had either lost his motivation or been frightened off by the involvement of the police.

She had received two follow-up visits from Constable Cheney. On the first he took her fingerprints so they could be matched against the prints found on the hypodermic and, on the second, he had told her that the forensic team had drawn a blank with their investigations on the hypodermic – the only prints on it were hers.

'Sorry,' Isabel had muttered, flushing as she imagined the resigned expression on Max Hawthorne's face when he got the news.

'It's easily done, handling things without thinking,' Constable Cheney reassured her. 'But Inspector Hawthorne has asked me to say that if you should receive anything else, could you please be very careful to handle it as little as possible?'

'I understand,' said Isabel gravely. 'It would be a most unwise woman who dared to go against Inspector Hawthorne's advice.'

PC Cheney had cleared his throat very noisily and hung about looking awkward for a few seconds. 'Well, work to be done!' he declared and stomped away up the steps in his thick, polished shoes.

As the week went by, Isabel found herself beginning to relax. Sometimes hours went by when she never gave a thought to the unknown man who had been fantasising about her. But just occasionally, even when absorbed at work, some small event or remark could trigger off the bad memories.

She had recently secured an account with a wealthy new client, who had been as slippery as a fish whilst he took his time deliberating on her investment proposals. He had openly told her he was taking advice from advisors in other companies and given her the impression that she would be damn lucky to get his business.

When he came to sign the contract, he had eyed her with lingering male appreciation and told her that of all the five advisors he had consulted, she was the only one who was not a complete waste of his time. 'Good to look at, as well,' he had commented. Isabel found his knowing grin and his offer of dinner that evening both patronising and offensive.

She had smiled at him, but there had been steel in her eyes. 'That's very kind of you. But I never mix business with pleasure.'

Undaunted, and with a fresh knowing smile, he had handed her a card giving his private number. 'Open invitation, Miss Bruce. Call me when you change your mind.'

Isabel showed him to the lift. As the doors closed and reduced him to a thin line, there was a sudden jarring thought that this unpleasant man could be the one – the man who sent letters and hypodermics and taxis for Highgate Cemetery.

That's ridiculous, she told herself as she walked back to her office.

Why should he? People who do that kind of thing are surely solitary, lonely people. This man ran a successful business, and was a member of numerous clubs and societies. But even so? What about his personal life? She knew nothing of that. He could be as lonely as hell.

Forget it, forget it! she told herself irritably, tidying the papers on her desk and taking them through into the adjoining office for her personal secretary to file. Forget the whole ghastly business.

And most of the time, she did.

On the Sunday of the following weekend, her half-sister, Luisa, was scheduled to arrive back in London. Her flight from Bangkok was due to land at six-fifteen in the evening and Isabel made sure to be at Heathrow in good time to meet her, knowing that Luisa would be exhausted from the long-haul flight.

The arrivals hall was teeming with passengers. Isabel amused herself trying to guess where they had come from. Some were in swinging winter coats, others in light anoraks. She guessed that the ones wearing shorts and sleeveless T-shirts to show off their new tans must have flown back from equatorial regions, and must surely be freezing in London's February greyness.

In time, she spotted Luisa coming towards her, her fashionably cut blonde hair falling over one eye as she bent to straighten a wobbling case on her trolley. 'Hi!' she called out as she looked up and saw Isabel. 'Oh, am I glad to see you!'

They hugged each other warmly. 'You're such an angel to come and meet me,' said Luisa. 'Bless you, darling.'

'How was the flight?' Isabel asked as they walked along together to the exit doors.

'Fairly horrendous. Some scary air turbulence,

followed by an hour of drunken football songs. You know...Oh dear, I really must stop being such a complaining cow.'

Isabel looked at her half-sister with affection and a stab of concern. Luisa had always been stick thin, but this evening she loooked gaunt, almost emaciated. There were dark smudges under her eyes and her delicate-boned face was lined with strain. She was wearing baggy grey combat trousers and a crumpled dark green fleece, and yet, thought Isabel, she still she managed to look fabulous. Luisa had such a sure sense of style that anything she put on always worked perfectly.

'How is your mother?' Isabel asked.

'Still going strong. As irrational and impossible as usual. By the time I'd been with her for three days, I was nearly chewing the chair legs. Be sure to tell me if I ever give the slightest sign of growing like her,' she concluded, rolling her eyes in mock horror at the very thought.

They stepped out into the chill air and Luisa shivered. 'February in London,' she groaned. 'I'd forgotten how bleak and dreary it is.'

Back at Isabel's flat, Luisa bombarded her with presents she had bought whilst waiting for the connection in Bangkok. Dior fragrances, fine wines and malt whisky from the duty-free shop. A cream silk nightdress, an emerald pashmina scarf, a tiny evening bag made of glinting tublar beads. Luisa was one of the world's big spenders and immensely generous.

Isabel had prepared a simple supper of spaghetti with tuna and lemon, served with a rocket and parmesan salad.

'This is so good,' Luisa said appreciatively. She looked up and smiled at Isabel. 'You're so talented, Isabel, it's not fair. Great dress sense, fabulous flair for interior decoration, a frighteningly brainy job. And you can cook!'

'You don't do so badly yourself.' Isabel reflected on Luisa's success over the past twenty years as a TV actress, both in Britain and Australia. She had only ever had the occasional long spell out of work and, during those periods, there had always been work doing voice-overs for advertisements which had kept her income buoyant. 'What's next in the offing?' she asked.

'Precious little.' Luisa took a long sip of wine. 'The smart young chick roles have all dried up, and the thirty-something parts are getting a bit more problematic.'

'Surely not.' Isabel looked hard at her sister, she was still gorgeous even though her fortieth birthday was rolling up fast.

'Oh yeah, it's true. I did two auditions while I was in Sydney. Both times I was pipped at the post by younger actresses. That's how the business works.' She observed her spaghetti thoughtfully as she wound it around her fork. 'I've got rehearsals coming up in March for a TV film, a psychological thriller, being put out in the autumn. Second female lead. And after that...well, who knows?'

Isabel stared at Luisa in fresh concern. 'Are you worried about it?'

Luisa shrugged. 'It's simply life, isn't it? Life as an actress, at any rate. You have success when you're young, everyone loves you. You get older. You get the character parts, and then the fillers in costume dramas, and by the time you're fifty, you've become more or less invisible – except for playing grannies.'

'Oh, come on!' Isabel chided. 'You're a long way off that.'

Luisa gave a wry smile. She looked at Isabel conspiratorially and narrowed her eyes. 'Let's talk about you. Tell me, how's your love life?'

'Quiet. In fact, non-existent.'

'It can't be true. Surely you must meet hosts of lovely men in that high-profile job of yours?'

Isabel shook her head. 'Most of them are rather old – and decidedly short on loveliness.'

'Well, what about the ones around in your social life? Parties and so on?'

Isabel considered recent parties she had been to, going along from a sense of politeness rather than inclination. Dinner parties where you were paired off with a single or recently-divorced man who was clearly on the lookout. The results invariably ranged from the embarrassing to the grim. Maybe the 'standing up drinking wine' scenario was marginally better, but then one was constantly in danger of being bored to death by men talking about the state of English football or their new computer!

The last party of that sort she had been to had been a typical disaster. She had known hardly anyone there, and had wandered from room to room holding a drink and pretending to be on her way to somewhere important.

'No luck there either. You've no need to worry Luisa, I'm quite content to wait until Mr Very Right Indeed comes strolling along. As everyone tells me he's bound to do.'

Luisa laid down her fork and dabbed her mouth on her napkin. She had eaten hardly anything, merely pushed her food around the plate.

'What's the matter, Luisa?' Isabel asked softly.

Luisa drained her wine. 'I'm pregnant,' she said flatly. 'Can you believe it? I nearly had a fit when the test was positive. Caught out at my age. What sort of fool does that make me?'

'Oh, Luisa!'

'Don't give me that reproachful little sister look,' Luisa told Isabel, giving a wry smile.

'You could go ahead and have it,' Isabel suggested, dismayed at the prospect of Luisa going through yet another abortion.

'No. No way. I need to keep in work and a bump isn't the best thing to be humping around with you at auditions.'

'Who's the father?'

'A producer I was auditioning for in London before I went to Australia.' Luisa looked hard at Isabel assessing her reaction. 'Hey, don't worry, sweetie. I haven't gone so low as to have to sleep my way into parts. We just fancied each other at the end of rather drunken party, and ended up in bed. He was a pretty dismal lover and he'd make a pretty dismal father.'

'What a mess,' Isabel said quietly.

'Exactly. Especially as I've just started a thing with a really lovely new guy.'

Isabel stared at the regretful face of her half-sister and then they both burst out laughing.

'You're a wicked, shameless woman! Go on then,' Isabel urged, 'tell me about him.'

'He's a dishy hunk,' Luisa said, her eyes glinting coquettishly. 'Totally gorgeous! His name's Josh and he's so nice. I can't believe my luck. He's only twenty-nine, so I've told him I'm thirty-four. And I haven't mentioned former husbands numbers one and two yet.'

'You lying cradle-snatcher, you.' Isabel teased.

Luisa gave a foxy smile. 'He tells me he's always liked older women. It's probably a mother complex or something. Well, so what? He's perfect for me.'

'So how long has this been going on?'

'Just a few weeks. I met him out in Sydney, where he was designing the set for a new play. Fantastically gifted. We got on famously together right from the word go, but he had to come back to London sooner than I did.'

Isabel got up and took the plates through to the kitchen, smiling to herself. Luisa's various men were always perfect for her. To start with at least!

As Isabel lifted cream from the fridge to serve with the apricot tart she had made the day before, she heard a little slapping sound on the tiles behind the main door. Her stomach twisted. She closed her eyes briefly. Oh no! Not another letter. But when she glanced through into the hallway, sure enough there was a brown envelope on the tiles. An envelope with a black rim.

Feeling sick, she ran into the hall, grasped the letter and stuffed it inside the telephone directory she kept on the little walnut table that had once belonged to her grand-mother.

She stared at the door, trying to imagine the person who had come softly down her steps and slid the envelope through the letter-box. It struck her that if she had been swift enough she might have been able to catch a glimpse of whoever it was from her front window. But now it was too late. It would have taken only seconds for the 'postman' to run up her steps into the road.

Isabel wanted to be strong, but she was alarmed to find herself in danger of bursting into tears. Her legs felt liquid and wobbly as she walked to the kitchen to get the apricot tart and the whipped cream.

Placing the tart on the table, Isabel noticed Luisa glance briefly up at her. She smiled, desperately trying to appear normal and relaxed, praying Luisa hadn't seen how violently her fingers were trembling. At least she was pretty sure Luisa hadn't heard anything, either on the steps or in the hallway. Isabel had put on a CD of Cole Porter songs earlier on, and Ella Fitzgerald's voice had been throbbing in the background as they ate, and was still going strong.

'When am I going to meet him? This new man – Josh?' Isabel wondered, handing Luisa a slice of tart. She wanted to keep the conversation firmly away from her own concerns.

'I'll fix something up,' Luisa said. 'We'll all have lunch together. Somewhere really nice.'

'Have you told him about the baby?'

Luisa gave a grimace.

'Forget it,' said Isabel. 'Ask a silly question.'

'I don't want him to know a thing about it, or its wretched father. That's why I'm going to rid of it as soon as possible.' Luisa pushed the tart away. 'Sorry, can't eat any more. It was sweet of you to bake for me, but I just feel so queasy all the time.' She ran her hands through her hair. 'Oh Lord, I'm sorry I'm being such a wet rag.'

Isabel got up and put her arms around Luisa. 'I love you big sister,' she said.

'Me too,' murmured Luisa, squeezing Isabel's arm. She looked up at her, her eyes thoughtful. 'Are you all right, darling Izzie? You're looking a bit…I don't know, under the weather.'

'Too much work, not enough play,' Isabel said lightly. She went off to the kitchen to make coffee and take some deep, calming breaths.

They drank their coffee and talked some more, but Luisa resisted Isabel's invitation to stay the night and called a taxi to take her and her luggage to an address in Clerkenwell.

'Is that where Josh lives?' Isabel asked, wishing most fervently that Luisa would have stayed on. Suddenly she was terribly afraid to be alone. She had a dread that after she had looked at the contents of the envelope, she would spend the night listening out for every tiny sound. Every creak of the house, every minute breath of wind shaking the branches of the trees in the street. Footsteps. Coming down her steps, nearer and nearer.

'Mmm. Can't wait to see him,' Luisa said. 'You don't mind,darling, do you? It was so lovely of you to come and fetch me, but…'

'No, of course you must go.'

Later on, she watched as Luisa walked up the steps, her elegant gazelle-like legs disappearing into the waiting taxi.

Alone, Isabel mechanically cleared away the plates and dishes and set the dishwasher going.

She double-checked the windows and doors, making absolutely sure they were secure. Then she moved to the desk, slid the envelope from its hiding place in the phone book and stared at it with mounting unease.

Maybe she could simply throw it in the bin? Or, alternatively, tear it into shreds and burn it in the sink? But somehow the need to know what it contained was an imperative, something over which she had no control, no choice. To know the worst was marginally better than allowing her imagination free rein.

Automatically, she took up the small silver dagger that had belonged to her grandmother and had been used by that delicate, dry little woman to open countless envelopes. But then she laid it down again. It seemed an insult to use that delicate antique instrument on such potentially vile correspondence.

Instead she prised open a small gap in the stuck-down flap of the envelope and made a small rent in it. Then she slid her index finger inside and let it work its way steadily along the fold, tearing a long slit the length of the envelope. Standard procedure for opening letters.

She had already torn most of the way along before she felt any pain. She was simply aware of a gleam of greyish-blue metal and a sense of puzzlement at the strange sticky feeling of the paper. It was moist and warm. And splattered with blood.

Then, suddenly, there was sharp, searing sensation in her right hand. She looked down and it took several seconds to understand what she was seeing. There was blood all over the place, bright splashes on her cream shirt, vivid speckles on the floor.

She looked again at the envelope, staring into the inside of the flap. There were something small and flat neatly taped there. A thin piece of shiny metal! Slowly, in horrified disbelief, she recognised it as a razor-blade that had been cut in half. One which would fit an old fashioned razor, the kind her father used for his morning shave. The sharp edge had been positioned in just the right place to slice into the finger that pushed open the flap.

She let out a yelp and dropped the envelope as though it were on fire. She looked at her hand and saw that the index finger was spurting out blood. Suddenly the pain of the cut was jabbing and intense and Isabel felt herself shiver, waves of hot and cold washing over her. Her legs buckled and she sank down on to the floor.

Somehow she managed to open the phone book, to dial the number of the local police station.

'Inspector Max Hawthorne,' she gasped. 'Now. This minute. Please!'

chapter five

He was there in less than ten minutes, calling to her through the door. 'Miss Bruce, Isabel, can you hear me? It's Max Hawthorne. Open the door, Isabel. You're safe now. Open the door.'

Shaking violently, she somehow managed to stand up and pull open the door. As he walked in she swayed and he caught her to him, holding her for a moment before he steered her into the kitchen and held her hand under running cold water.

She couldn't stop trembling and when she spoke her voice was jerky, coming out in little gasping bursts. 'It was in the envelope,' she said, 'A razor-blade.' She watched in fascination as the water flowed over her fingers and pinky streams disappeared into the plughole. 'Who would do this?' she asked in bewilderment.

'I'm taking you to Casualty,' he said. 'That cut needs checking over by a doctor.' He bound up her hand with wads of kitchen roll then helped her into her coat and half-guided, half-carried her up the steps and helped her into his car.

On the drive to the hospital, she vaguely registered his calling into the station to report what had happened, requesting that a female officer meet them at the hospital.

She sat beside him in silence, unable to fully take in what had just happened to her. For the first minutes after she had cut herself, she had been numb with dismay and disbelief, but now her hand began to throb with pain.

Through a haze of shock, she felt Max Hawthorne propel her to the admissions desk where he demanded she be seen instantly. Within seconds she was in a small curtained cubicle where her wound was thoroughly inspected, cleaned and then bandaged by a brisk young woman doctor.

'Razor cuts are always nasty,' she told Isabel. 'And very painful, so I'm going to give you some pills which will take the edge off the hurting.'

Max Hawthorne was waiting as she left the cubicle and there was a uniformed policewoman with him. She had dark hair scraped back from her face, and a stern, unbending expression. She nodded briefly to Isabel, and she and Hawthorne flicked a curious glance at her bandaged hand.

'I'm all right,' Isabel told them, stepping out determinedly down the corridor, willing her legs to be firm and steady.

Back at her flat, Max settled Isabel on the sofa and asked the policewoman, who he introduced as Sergeant Emma Hayes, to go into the kitchen to make tea.

'I'll do it,' Isabel said, making a move to stand up.

'No, you won't,' he said. 'Just relax.'

She looked up at him. 'Easier said than done,' she said, her glance faintly challenging.

'Yes, I know.'

'Do you? Well, I suppose you've seen all this before. Happening to other people. But experiencing it, being the *victim,* is something quite different.' The word victim rang in her head and she wished she hadn't said it. Saying it made it true. She *had* become a victim. Passive and helpless. A target.

'I'm sorry,' he said softly.

Sergeant Hayes came in with the tea. Solemnly, she placed a steaming mug on the low table in front of the sofa just within Isabel's reach.

'Aren't you having one?' Isabel asked, looking from one to the other.

'We're not guests,' Hawthorne said tersely.

'No, but this is my flat and I'm not in the habit of sitting around drinking tea without offering some to anyone who happens to be here with me.'

She saw a glance pass between Hawthorne and the Sergeant. He gave a curt nod and Emma Hayes returned to the kitchen.

'Are you fit to answer a few questions?' Hawthorne asked.

'I suppose so.'

'Miss Bruce,' he said gravely, 'I do appreciate what a bad time this is for you. I'll be very brief.'

She gave an ironic smile. 'And then you'll be back first thing in the morning.'

'This is all for your safety,' he pointed out.

'I know. And I'm grateful for you coming tonight, and so quickly. Go on.'

Sergeant Hayes returned with two further mugs of tea. She gave one to Hawthorne who instantly set it down on the table as though it were an irritating distraction.

'May I see the envelope you received tonight?' Hawthorne asked.

Isabel winced at the memory. 'It's on the hall table. No, I think I dropped it on the floor. There's blood everywhere,' she said, recalling those few terrible moments as she opened the envelope.

Hawthorne gave Emma Hayes another curt nod. She went out and quickly returned, carrying the envelope.

Isabel noticed that she had pulled on a thin glove and was holding the blood spattered paper very gingerly.

Hawthorne took it from her, holding it by a tiny tip at the corner. He laid it on the table, then took some small tweezers from his pocket and prised the envelope open again. After staring at it thoughtfully for a few moments, he bent his head to look inside. Slowly he inserted the tweezers and pulled out a folded piece of paper.

'Oh, God!' Isabel exclaimed, 'not another letter.'

'It would seem so.' He looked at her, his face grim. 'Do you want me to read it?'

'Yes,' she whispered.

Slowly he unfolded the paper and absorbed its contents. Isabel saw his mouth tighten. 'Do you want me to read it to you?'

'No. Oh, I don't know.' She stared at him in appeal as she struggled to decide. 'Yes. Not knowing is worse than anything.'

'I agree with you.' He began to read in a flat, emotion-stripped voice. *'"Dear Isabel, Are you getting jumpy yet? Just a little, maybe? I think so. Do you look around when you go out walking? Do you listen out in the night for footsteps? You should, you know. I'm not quite sure what I'm going to do with you yet. But if I were you, I'd check your door is locked and the windows fastened. There are so many wicked people around these days, isn't that so?"'*

A deep hollow seemed to open up in Isabel's stomach. Instinctively, she wrapped her arms around herself in a geture of protection. Pain seared through her injured hand and her eyes felt hot and burning. She had to make a huge effort not to cry. I must be strong, she told herself. 'That is grim,' she said in a low, flat voice. 'Horrible.'

She reached out and picked up her mug of tea. Her hand trembled so violently, that fat drops of warm liquid sloshed over the rim and fell on to her skirt. As she attempted to replace the mug on the table, Hawthorne reached out and gently prised it from her shaking fingers. 'Take your time,' he said, 'take deep breaths.'

After a few moments he spoke again, his voice low and gentle now. 'Is this letter like the others?'

Isabel considered. 'Not really. No.'

'What makes you say that?'

'The others were far more...personal.'

There was a pause. Please don't ask me to elaborate, Isabel prayed silently, looking from the Inspector to his Sergeant. Not with that young woman there, listening and judging. Isabel felt she might just be able to bring herself to tell Max Hawthorne in private, for despite his stern, unbending manner he had a strange knack of creating an atmosphere of trust. But she needed to be alone with him in order to confide. She couldn't speak while Emma Hayes and her hard eyes were watching.

'Do you think this last letter was written by a different person?' Hawthorne asked, leaning forward, his eyes sharpening with speculation.

'No.' Isabel glanced up at him. 'The envelope is identical to the others. There surely can't be more than one person who buys brown envelopes, outlines them in black ink and sends them to unsuspecting women.'

'You think this person might be targeting other people besides you?' Hawthorne asked, glancing swiftly at Sergeant Hayes who was carefully recording the conversation in a lined notebook.

'No, I don't,' Isabel said fiercely. 'I feel what this man is doing is horribly personal. That it's just me he's interested in, just me who's suffering. I expect most people who get hate mail feel equally paranoid.'

There was a silence. They think I'm neurotic and hysterical, thought Isabel wearily.

'I think you need to rest now,' Max Hawthorne told her. 'I'm going to go back to the station to organise for a watch to be kept outside your flat. Sergeant Hayes will stay here with you until another officer comes to join her.'

'Will that be long?' Isabel asked, 'I'd like to go to bed.'

'Not long at all, and you can go to bed when you like. Sergeant Hayes won't interfere with whatever you want to do.'

Yes she will, thought Isabel. It was not really anything personal against Emma Hayes, even though Isabel found it hard to warm to the grave-faced Sergeant. It was the whole terrifying notion that she, Isabel Bruce, was now a poor victim who needed police protection. She felt like a marked woman. Her freedom and her self-respect were gradually being stripped away from her.

She got up. She knew she had to fight with every ounce of her strength not to give in to this unknown person who was trying to intimidate and manipulate her. Already he had changed the routine of her life, but she was damned if he was going eat into her independence, into the very heart of her. 'I'm going to make some fresh tea,' she told the Inspector crisply. 'I shall be able to manage to do it perfectly well on my own and I'll take it to bed and drink it whilst I'm listening to the radio. And then I shall go to sleep.'

Max Hawthorne's cool eyes connected with hers. 'Good,' he said. 'That's the way to play it.' He watched her, his gaze calm and focused as though there were no other thoughts in his head but her. She was suddenly reminded of the way his image had crept into her dreams on that first night she had met him. Her stomach gave a sudden lurch and prickles of awareness rippled across her scalp under her hair.

'Goodnight then,' she said formally, glancing first at Sergeant Hayes and then at Max Hawthorne.

'I shall need to speak to you tomorrow,' he said. He seemed to take it for granted that her time was completely at his disposal and Isabel was in no mood to be bossed around. Not even by this dignified and powerful man who was, after all, simply doing his job.

'I have a number of important appointments tomorrow,' she told him. 'I shall be at my office and I have a very heavy schedule. It's Monday tomorrow. People work on a Monday.' She heard the words echoing in the short silence that followed. She knew she must have sounded sarcastic and negative, but she hadn't meant it like that. Her words were more a plea for normality than anything else. She simply wanted things to be ordinary again, to carry on with her life.

She looked pleadingly at Max Hawthorne, uncomfortably aware that it was now late on a Sunday evening and that both he and Emma Hayes were still hard at work. Working on her – Isabel's – behalf, to help her and keep her safe. And it didn't look as though they had much chance of an early finish. 'I'm sorry,' she said

Suddenly she felt utterly exhausted as though if she didn't lie down immediately she would simply collapse. Tears were queuing up to be shed again. She would not cry, she would *not,* she told herself.

Max Hawthorne was still gazing at her. And then, quite unexpectedly, he gave a slow smile of such understanding, such concern, such sweetness, that her breath stopped in her chest and the room around her seemed to fade to a blur.

'Goodnight,' she muttered, and half-stumbled, half-ran from the room, straight to her bedroom and shut the door.

Emma Hayes raised her eyebrows. 'She's in a real state, sir. Who wouldn't be?'

'Exactly.' He paused, reflecting. 'I don't think we should discuss the case now, Sergeant. Not here, we don't want to upset her further. I'll catch up with you in the morning. Meantime make a record of every angle you can think of, and anything you notice, however trivial.'

'Yes sir.'

Max got into his car and started the engine. He was extremely worried. He was still not sure whether Isabel Bruce's case had a link with the other two local young women who had been attacked. But this new development in Isabel's case, this cruel form of harassment using a razor, seemed particularly sinister. Whether it was connected to the other cases or not, it made him deeply concerned for her safety.

And there was something else. Something crazy and puzzling and totally unexpected – something quite unrelated to his concerns about her as a professional. His feelings had become involved.

It had been four years since Jennifer died and, during those years, his life had been stripped of love, affection and passion. He had invited one or two women colleagues out to dinner but nothing had come of it. His heart seemed cold and lifeless. He had learned to comfort himself with the satisfaction of his work.

But there was something about Isabel Bruce that moved him and stirred up feelings long ago abandoned. Her physical presence made him feel alive again and set his senses humming. He admired her courage and her determination. But beneath her strength, he sensed a deep vulnerability and an essential femininity which made him want to fold her to him and keep her very close.

She's the victim of a crime, he reminded himself. A potential key witness in an important investigation. He must keep his distance.

chapter six

Isabel slept fitfully, woke at five and stared up at the ceiling for a long time. The hands of her watch crawled as though they were held back by ropes.

At six she got up and peered out of the window. At the top of the roadshe could see a police car, but she couldn't see the face of the officer. She hoped it wasn't Sergeant Hayes, the poor woman would be exhausted by now.

She went into the bathroom and locked the door, leaning against it for a moment. She splashed cold water on her face with her left hand and then noticed that tiny specks of blood were seeping through the muslin bandage on her injured hand. When she took a shower, she had to wrap a hand towel around it to keep it dry.

Having her right hand trussed up and out of use made everything so difficult. Putting on her make-up was something of a challenge – she eventually abandoned any attempt to use a mascara wand, and simply patted a little grey shadow over her eye sockets. She then noticed that the shadow matched the dark smudges of fatigue below her eyes and rubbed if off again. A little moisturiser and some lip gloss would have to do.

It took twice as long as usual to dress, but eventually she was ready. Navy suit, cream shirt, black high heels. She let herself out of the house and walked down the street, wondering if she should make some acknowledgement to the officer inside the police car. In the end she simply walked past it, looking back at her house instead, wondering if Flo might be at her window to give a cheery wave. But there was no sign of the old lady. She had probably given up waiting for Isabel to leave, she was so late this morning.

The buses were crowded and she had to stand for the whole journey, strap-hanging with her left hand because the right was beginning to throb again.

'Sorry I'm late,' she told her assistant, Esther, who was clearly surprised to have arrived at work before her boss.

'Hey, what have you done to yourself?' Esther exclaimed, spotting Isabel's bandage.

'A cut,' Isabel said swiftly. 'Sliced myself on the food processor blade.'

'Ooh! They're terrible things. Lethal,' Esther said sympathetically. 'You should take care.'

Isabel gave a wry smile. 'I certainly will.'

'I've opened the morning post and put it on your desk,' Esther said. 'Don't think there's anything too drastic!'

Isabel stared at her, suddenly thinking how dreadful it would be if the hate-mailer decided to target her at work. If Esther should open some ghastly missive and find out what was going on. Or get hurt. Oh God!

'Are you all right?' Esther asked, concerned. 'You're very pale. Shall I bring you some coffee?'

Isabel nodded. 'That would be lovely.'

She walked through to her office and began to leaf through the morning post, cursing her left hand for being so inept. Reading through the mail, she found that she had to force herself to concentrate. Her eyes skimmed the print but didn't seem to send any messages to her brain, and she had to read things all over again.

Esther brought in the coffee and handed Isabel her desk diary. 'You've got a team meeting in twenty minutes. Do you want me to get out the papers you'll be needing?'

'Yes.' Isabel looked at her assistant and smiled gratefully. Esther was only seventeen and had been with the firm for less than two months. She always dressed in bright, happy colours and had a fondness for tight, short little tops and tight, short little skirts with her bare midriff peeping out. Isabel recalled that she had been planning to drop some tactful hints about airing the midriff in the office. Forget it! What did it matter? 'You're such a thoughtful assistant, Esther,' she said impulsively.

'Oh!' said Esther, looking extremely startled and then pleased. 'Well, thanks!'

Isabel sipped her coffee and tried to focus her thoughts on the coming meeting. She would need all her wits about her as the team were bright, experienced people who expected quality leadership, and the Monday morning planning meeting always set the tone for the week.

She tried to force her mind to work efficiently, but it was skittering all over the place, flitting from one anxious conjecture to another. Not one of them relating to work.

Five minutes before the meeting, she went into her small private bathroom, smoothed her hair and put on some red lipstick. Bold lipstick was usually a big confidence-giver, but today it looked all wrong, like a gash of blood in her drained, white face. She wiped it off with a tissue, then made her way to the conference room.

Her team was all assembled and Esther was ready with a notebook and pen. They looked up as she came in, their faces welcoming but strangely curious. With a jolt of unease she glanced at her watch. She was ten minutes late. She was *never* late. What had she been doing all that time in the bathroom? Staring, unseeing into the mirror, she supposed.

Take a grip, she told herself, turning to the first item on the agenda.

Twenty minutes into the meeting she judged she was doing reasonably well. It was a huge effort to concentrate but she thought she would just about manage to make it to the end of the hour, providing no unforseen problems cropped up. Not more than a few seconds later, she saw the door open and one of the firm's senior partners walk in. There was something in his face as he came towards her that made her stop in mid-sentence.

Bending towards her, he murmured tersely in her ear. 'You're wanted in reception Isabel. It's the police, CID. I'll take over here.'

'Can't they come back later?' Suddenly she felt icy cold all over.

'You must go now.' His eyes flicked over her face, eyes filled with questioning, with cold suspicion as to what one of his departmental managers had been up to in order to attract such urgent attention from the police.

'Right.' She stood up. 'I'm sorry,' she said, glancing around her curious colleagues, 'I'll be back as soon as I can.'

Riding the lift down to reception she took deep breaths to calm herself. Max Hawthorne was standing just inside the entry door, his eyes already fixing on her as the lift doors slid apart. He didn't smile or make any gesture, but his gaze was so intense it was as if he were physically pulling her towards him. She felt a sudden jolt of pure magnetic sensation.

He looked as though he hadn't slept. There was a dark shadow around his cheeks and jaw and his eyes were dulled with weariness. He was the last man in the world she had wanted to see that morning…and the only man she wanted to see. The blood pulsed in her neck and her face.

Get a grip, she told herself once again, furious to find herself thrown off balance like this. 'Why have you come here? Couldn't this wait?' she asked the Inspector coldly. 'You've pulled me out of a very important meeting.'

'We need to go somewhere private to talk,' he informed her, his face calm and emotionless. 'I could drive you home or we could go to the station.'

'I can't just walk out of my job during work hours. I've got important meetings and appointments. Why didn't you telephone first..?' She knew there was no point in protesting. But something drove her to assert herself, after all, that was the way she was used to behaving. That was what her management courses had taught her. You didn't have tantrums, you didn't lose your temper, you simply made quiet, firm statements of what you were and were not prepared to do. And then you stuck by what you'd decided.

'This can't wait,' he cut in harshly.

'Why not?'

'Because,' he said, his lips tight with irritation, 'this is about trying to catch some obsessive criminal out there who is determined to do harm to innocent women. And the next one on the list could well be you.'

Isabel gasped with dismay. 'Oh God! Have you found out something new? Has something awful happened?'

'No one else has been assaulted but there *is* a new development. And this is not the place to discuss it,' he said meaningfully.

She sighed. 'All right.'

He held the door for her as she climbed into his car. 'Please tell me what's going on,' she demanded as she clipped on her seat belt.

'There's been another suspicious letter delivered to your house.'

'What? You mean by hand?' She jerked forward in her seat. 'Well, why didn't you arrest the person who delivered it? Charge him or whatever?'

'The letter came through the post,' he said patiently. 'We intercepted the postman when he brought the morning delivery. We took possession of the suspect envelope and he posted the others through your letter box as normal.'

'Are you allowed to do that? I thought the mail was sacrosanct. Sort of State property.'

He gave a little smile. 'Oh, yes, we have authority to do that. We're an arm of the State as well.'

She winced at her stupidity. 'Yes, of course. So what's in this latest letter?' Her mouth dried. She waited for his reply, tense and miserable.

'I haven't opened it. But I can guess what's in it.'

'Where is it?'

'In my jacket pocket.'

'Let me see it.'

'Not while we're driving.'

'It's not a bomb, is it? I want to see it *now*. It's mine after all.'

'You can see it when we get back to your flat.'

The fight suddenly went out of her. She sat back in her seat, silent and leaden with foreboding.

He pushed open the door as she turned the key. The morning mail slithered across the tiles and Isabel picked up the envelopes. There was a letter from her father, an electricity account, and an advertising leaflet for a new Greek restaurant which had just opened in the High Street.

'Do you want coffee?' she asked Max Hawthorne. 'I certainly do. Strong and black.'

He nodded and wandered off into the-sitting room. When she brought the tray through he was examining a photograph of her and her father, taken on a holiday in Rome eight years before. He placed the frame carefully back in the exact spot it had been before.

'You open it,' she told him, as she watched him slide one of the now familiar brown envelopes from the inner pocket of his jacket. 'And be careful.'

'There's no metal inside. I've checked,' he said drily. He took a penknife from his pocket, opened it and slit the top of the envelope with one neat stroke. He looked inside, then tore a clean sheet from his notebook and placed it on the coffee table. Carefully and deftly he shook the contents of the envelope onto the paper.

Isabel stared in disbelief. There on the paper lay one single lock of hair. A shining russet curl around six inches long. A curl so similar to those of her own she automatically she put a hand up to touch her hair. Surely no one could have cut such a thick strand from it without her noticing. She glanced at Max Hawthorne who was looking thoughtfully at the shorn curl as though it were an exhibit of some kind. She supposed that was what it was, as far as he was concerned. 'Oh God, this is awful, grotesque,' she cried.

He nodded. She looked again at the hair. 'It's not mine,' she told him.

'Are you sure?'

'Absolutely. It can't be!' She reached across, impelled to touch the hair, to discover that it did not have the feel of hers. He put out a hand and stopped her. Their fingers touched.

'It's definitely not mine. It's not quite the same colour.' She knew she sounded desperate and melodramatic but the so badly wanted the hair not to be hers. 'You must do some DNA testing or whatever it is you do.'

Still he watched her. Silent, impassive, judgemental.

She tugged viciously at two or three strands of hair on the crown of her head and tore them out. 'Here, take these to your forensic people so they can compare them.'

He frowned and then his expression changed to one of pure human sympathy and concern.

'Don't!' she shouted at him. 'Don't pity me as if I'm a wounded animal or under some kind of curse. I don't want pity. Just find the wretched person behind all this and lock him up.'

'There's nothing I'd like to do better,' he said quietly. 'And that's why I need you to help me.'

She settled herself down. 'All right, fair enough. I'll try to be calm and rational, but it's not easy. This kind of thing changes you into a different person.'

'Yes, I understand.'

'Do you?' She opened her eyes wide in challenge. 'I wonder. You'll be able to walk away from all this when you leave my house. You'll be able to go safely back to your office and write up everything I say in neat precise notes, and then plan some ingenious campaign of detection. You won't have to live with the idea of some unknown person tracking your moves, someone who hates you and wants to keep on hurting you.'

'You're quite wrong,' he cut in. 'I won't be able to walk away from it, not until we've caught this person. And it's my responsibility to do just that. And fast. That's why you've got to work with me to find him, Isabel.'

She swallowed. 'Yes, all right then. What is it you

want to know?'

'We'll need to go through your diaries – personal and work – and your address book. Also, I need to know about any recent correspondence or conversations with family and friends.'

'We?' she echoed. 'Who exactly will be looking through my private things? Besides you?' Her eyes were fierce as she spoke, but he didn't flinch. It struck her that he always met her gaze openly and directly and she liked that, it was genuine and honest – or did it simply mean he was trying to catch her out?

'My team,' he said.

Isabel thought of pink-faced Constable Jack Cheney and iron-faced Sergeant Emma Hayes. She wondered who else. She imagined them quoting entries from her diaries and joking and laughing about them. To do that was only human nature, after all. 'Oh!'

'Is that a problem?'

'I'd rather it were just you. I don't know your team. How do I know I can trust them?'

There was a silence. She bowed her head. 'Forget that, Inspector Hawthorne. Just get on and do what you need to do to end this nightmare.'

'Isabel,' he said gently, 'I'll try to make this as easy as possible, and I'll try to guard those…aspects of your life which are very private and sensitive.'

'I know, I believe you. My diaries are in here in the house. You're welcome to look. You'll have to phone my assistant Esther for my work schedules. Oh, and I suppose you'll want me to stay here and answer more questions, so please tell her I won't be in the office again until tomorrow. You're free to say whatever you like as the reason.'

He looked at her and nodded gravely. 'Very well. Thank you for that.'

'So what else do you want to know?'

'We need a record of all the people you've had contact with recently. Friends, colleagues, clients…'

'Hairdresser, beauty therapist, dentist,' she suggested ironically. 'The entire *dramatis personae* of my life!'

'We can't rule anyone out.'

He spent the next three hours reading through her diaries and correspondence. On occasions he would rap out terse requests for clarification on certain names and appointments, while Isabel sat numb and passive, giving flat mechanical answers to his questions.

Whilst working he was absorbed, his face harsh and frowning. She felt almost afraid of him, his concentration was so intense.

When it got to two o'clock she prepared cheese on toast, adding a dash of mustard and cream to the grated cheddar before she put it under the grill. He thanked her perfunctorily and ate automatically. as though simply putting fuel into his body and mind. From time to time he went out into the hallway and she could hear him talking in a low voice on his mobile phone. She presumed he was calling back to the station, consulting with his team.

At three o'clock Emma Hayes arrived. She smiled politely at Isabel, looking at her curiously for a few seconds as though she were an animal in a zoo. Isabel disappeared into the kitchen so that she and Hawthorne could talk freely. She was beginning to feel like a spare part, rather than the central character in this particular drama.

Emma Hayes left half an hour later, carrying Isabel's diaries and letters in clear plastic bags. When Isabel went back into the sitting-room, she noticed that both the mailed lock of hair and her own strands had been removed.

At four o'clock her house phone rang. She went into her bedroom to take the call.

'Izzie, darling – it's me!'

'Luisa, how are you?'

'Could be worse. But what about you? I rang work and they told me you were off sick. Are you OK sweetie?'

'Yes.' She thought frantically of a way to reassure her sister. 'Just a tummy upset, I'll be fine tomorrow.'

'It's not like you going down with a bug. I'm the fragile one!' Luisa said giving a dry laugh. 'Listen, darling, I'm having the abortion tomorrow.'

'Oh, Luisa!'

'Don't! Don't try to persuade me against it. I've made up my mind. Just say a little prayer for me.'

Isabel took down the address and phone number of the private clinic in Hampstead where Luisa had booked in. 'I'll come to take you home,' she said. 'Get them to ring me when you can come out.'

'No. It's OK, darling. Josh is coming to get me. I've come clean with him, told him the whole sorry story.'

'Was that a good idea? What did he say?'

'That he still adores me, the crazy man.'

Isabel put the phone down, frowning in thought.

As she went back into the sitting-room, Max Hawthorne fixed her with his penetrating gaze.

'That was my sister Luisa,' she said, feeling an explanation was needed.

'I see.'

'Just a family call.'

He nodded, his face stern and full of conjecture.

Isabel felt guilty, as though she were under suspicion of lying. Hell! That couldn't be right.

'I'm going back to the station now,' he said and she found herself feeling alarmed and disconcerted. It was as though he were whipping a safety net from under her. With him close by, at least she felt safe, even though he was a not the easiest of presences. She realised the house would feel empty and hollow without him. Dear God! What was happening to her? She must be falling apart.

'There'll be an officer outside watching the house all the time. You'll be quite safe.'

'Will I?'

'Yes,' he said softly.

'When are you coming back?' she demanded before she could stop herself.

'This evening.' He hesitated. 'We need to talk things through. There's a proposition I want to put to you.'

Suddenly Isabel's humour broke through. 'A proposition Inspector! You sound like a hero in a Jane Austen novel.'

He didn't smile and his solemn stare made her feel as though she had been silly and frivolous. 'I'm afraid I don't quite measure up to the romantic hero image,' he said flatly. At the door he turned and mechanically issued the now familiar warnings about security and safety.

As he went up the steps, Isabel had a swift recall of the long hours they had spent together that day. All the questions he had asked, the information he had gathered about her life. Two weeks ago she had never set eyes on Max Hawthorne, but it struck her that the inscrutable Inspector probably now knew more about her than anyone else in the world.

chapter seven

'Any suggestions?' Max Hawthorne asked Constable Cheney and Sergeant Hayes when he had finished briefing them on the results of his trawl through Isabel's letters and diaries. The muscles of his face were tense and strained and shadows of fatigue showed as dark smudges beneath his eyes.

'The lock of hair is a clear indication of a link with the battering cases,' Emma Hayes said carefully.

'But the letters don't fit,' Jack Cheney observed. 'The Batterer" doesn't send messages. Could be dyslexic or whatever.'

'I don't think dyslexia is an issue, and I think you mean illiterate,' Emma Hayes said loftily, making the constable grimace with annoyance.

'I'm inclined to think we can't rule out a link,' Max said with a firmness that ended the squabble. 'Stalkers and harassers are well known for elaborating their tactics as they go along. So, staying with the theory that Isabel Bruce has attracted the attentions of the same person who targeted the other victims, I've got a suggestion to put to you as to how we might flush our batterer out.'

Both Cheney and Hayes snapped to attention. As they listened to their senior officer's low steady voice, their eyes widened with surprise. The constable looked rather excited but Emma Hayes was more cautious. 'Isn't that rather risky, sir?'

'Yes, Emma, it is. However, I think we can provide

Isabel Bruce with sufficient cover to minimise the risk to just the tiniest of odds that she'll be in danger.'

'What does the Super say?' Jack Cheney wondered. 'Have you tackled him yet?'

'I have and he's agreed. Authorised as much man and woman-power as I judge necessary.'

'Wow!' Jack said, staring at his boss with respect.

'He wants this case sewn up,' Max said. 'The press are already making some ugly noises about police incompetence.'

'Snide bunch!' was Jack's scornful comment.

'We shall have to rely on Isabel Bruce to be both discreet and very courageous,' Emma observed. 'Do you really think she's up to it, sir?'

Max treated his sergeant to a long level look. 'Yes Emma, I do. She strikes me as very strong, very spirited and resourceful – the kind of person friends would appeal to in a crisis. I don't think she's a woman to cave in easily.'

'She was a bag of twitching nerves last night,' said Emma looking sceptical.

'I think you would be too if you'd just had your fingers sliced with a razor blade from an anonymous sender,' Max responded with a note of chiding.

As he shrugged on his jacket and left the room, Emma Hayes knew she had been rebuked. Her face grew hot and pink. Max Hawthorne had the knack of being able to make you squirm with a mere altered inflection in his voice or a raised eyebrow. She'd rather have a good bawling out from the Superintendent any time.

Constable Cheney was watching her with interest.

'What? What's the matter?' Emma asked him crossly.

'Nothing. It's just struck me!'

'What has?'

'I've never heard the boss talk about a woman like that before. Or anyone else for that matter. He really admires her. In fact,' said Jack, warming to his new theory, 'I'd go so far as to say our cool-as-a-cucumber Inspector is a bit smitten. And good for him.'

'Rubbish. Sometimes you talk a load of hot air, Jack. What makes you think that?'

'Oh, I don't know Sarge,' said Jack with a superior manly smile. 'Just put it down to masculine intuition.'

Max Hawthorne went back to his flat in Central London just a few minutes walk from Tower Bridge. He showered, shaved and put on fresh clothes, then stood looking out of his window from where he could see the full, fast flow of the Thames. There had been a lot of rain in the past few days and this evening there was a stiff wind. The surface of the water was whipped up into seething whirls, the crests of each wave spiked with horns of silver from a frail crescent moon.

It would take him around twenty minutes to drive to Isabel's basement flat. He decided to take the tube for two stations, then walk the rest of the way. Hunched inside his navy overcoat, he tried to imagine what it would be like to be a woman on her own. Walking in the darkness, constantly looking over her shoulder to see if there was a figure following. An unknown male pursuer. Because in these kind of cases, it invariably was a man who was the pursuer; his prey a hapless, helpless female victim.

He heard the bare branches of the trees groan as they moved in the wind. The sound echoed eerily. It was not hard to imagine there were footsteps behind, the swish of a macintosh, the crunch of heels. What would it be like, he thought, frowning? To be tracked and pursued by someone bigger and stronger than you, someone of the other sex whose thought systems and motivations were subtly different from yours?

On the whole, totally terrifying and demoralising he decided.

Isabel opened the door before he rang the bell. Clearly she had been waiting for him. He noticed that she had changed from her office clothes into dove grey trousers and a coral pink angora sweater which clashed wonderfully with her russet hair.

She showed him through to the sitting-room, and he noticed that the table was set for two. A bottle of wine stood cooling in an antique silver wine bucket. He was touched. His heart sank.

'I know you're not supposed to fraternise or drink on duty,' she said with a dangerously bright smile. 'But I was suddenly starving and I suspect you are too. I've ordered a Chinese meal to be delivered in around twenty minutes. You can answer the door so I'm in no danger.'

'Who can argue with that?' he murmured, settling himself on her sofa.

'Will you open the wine?' she asked. 'I'm having difficulty doing it with my left hand.' She held out a corkscrew.

He jumped up. 'How is your hand?' he enquired, as he twisted the corkscrew into the cork.

'It stings. Quite a lot. I've thought about putting a new bandage on but it's really not at all easy to do anything complicated with one hand.'

'Shall I do it for you?'

She looked up at him. Her eyes were full of challenge, yet lit with a spark of humour. She was so beautiful, he just wanted to stand and gaze at her. 'No, Inspector. You won't,' she said. 'I'm fiercely independent about that sort of thing. I'll get my GP to change the dressing tomorrow.'

'Fine,' he said.

She poured the wine into tall glasses. 'Will you have some?'

He shook his head. 'Drinking on a duty is strictly forbidden. Sorry.'

His eyes connected with hers and a shivering current of connection flashed between them. Max quickly looked away, reminding himself to keep his distance.

The door buzzer rang. On a reflex, as though she were one of Pavlov's experimental dogs, Isabel registered a thrill of fear leap through her nerves.

Max got up to answer the door, while Isabel took a long sip of wine.

How long could she keep up this brave, jokey front, she asked herself. Inside she felt wretched; shredded and weak and fearful. And so tired she just wanted to stretch out somewhere very safe and sleep, sleep, sleep.

He came back holding a brown bag. 'The cartons inside look suspiciously like containers for Chinese food,' he said dryly. 'Would you like me to open them?'

She smiled. 'Shall we do it together?' She got plates from the kitchen as Max set the containers on the table and opened them one-by-one, peeling each white cardboard lid carefully from its foil enclosure. 'It all looks fine,' he said quietly.

'Did you truly think the food could have been tampered with?' Isabel asked, fresh dismay springing up.

'No, but it's always wise to be cautious.'

Isabel sighed.

'Eat something,' he urged her, looking up and seeing

her white, anxious face as she twiddled noodles around her fork. 'It's all very good.'

Isabel put a forkful of food into her mouth and forced herself to chew. She felt as though they were marking time, putting off the evil moment when they would have to get down to the nitty-gritty of Max Hawthorne's visit. She had the impression he was uneasy, like someone debating whether or not to divulge a secret.

They ate in silence. There was very little fraternising.

'Let's move away from the table,' he said, when it became clear neither of them had much interest in food.

He settled in a corner of the sofa and she chose one of her formal upright chairs. She realised it had been a mistake to treat Max Hawthorne like some kind of friend. He was here to do a job, and all she had achieved was to waste his time going through a pointless charade of pretending they could socialise with each other.

She sat stiff-backed, conscious that his eyes were on her – thoughtful and assessing. Eventually she could stand the suspense no longer. 'Go on then, Inspector. Tell me about it. Your proposition.'

He went on looking steadily at her. 'Before I do that, I'd like you to tell me about the letters,' he said briskly. 'Anything at all you can remember.'

She took a few moments to collect her thoughts. 'They were quite short to start with. "*I know where you live, I'm watching you*". That sort of thing. I suppose it's pretty standard stuff in these sort of cases?'

He gave no repsonse. 'Go on, please.'

'Then they got more scary. More – personal.' She paused.

'Would you rather tell this to a woman officer?' he enquired.

She thought of Emma Hayes's hard face and shook her head. 'I'm trying to remember the exact words.' That was not true, of course. She was simply playing for time. The problem was not remembering – the problem was forgetting.

Max Hawthorne waited, patient, calm, no emotion showing.

'There were remarks about my hair and how beautiful it was. And about my legs being long. And quite a lot about my breasts – how round and heavy they looked and how he would like to cup them in his hands.' She stopped, swallowed painfully, cleared her throat. 'And how he would like to tie me to the bed with satin ribbons, and part my legs and look at me.'

'You may find this observation bizarre and insensitive, but these sound almost like love letters,' Max suggested in a low voice.

'Yes, I can see why you say that but there was a lot about wanting to hurt me too. About the pleasure you can get from feeling pain. *"A kind of pleasure more intense than any you've known before",'* she quoted.

'Were those the exact words?'

'More or less.'

'The last letter I shredded was the worst. It was about watching my face when he took me to the limits of pain.' She stopped, she didn't think her voice would work any more. 'Do you think that was a death threat?' she asked, her voice barely audible.

'Possibly,' he said steadily. 'Although it sounds more like the threats of someone who gets an intense thrill simply from inflicting pain.'

'Yes.' She sighed and her body sagged. She felt that in asking for this information, Hawthorne had picked her up and turned her inside out.

'Isabel,' he said softly as though calling to her from a distance. 'That first night I came to visit you, I was fairly confident there was a link between the harassment you'd been experiencing and two recent episodes of assault on young women in this area.'

Her head jerked up. 'Oh God! What happened to them? Are they all right. Are they alive?'

'They're both alive. They were attacked in quiet back streets and their faces were brutally and savagely beaten.'

'Were they raped?' she asked in a flat voice.

'No. Their underclothes had been torn, but there was no evidence of rape.'

Shivers of horror ran up Isabel's spine. She sat hunched as though in self-protection, her unbandaged left hand kneading her right arm. Now she felt as if she'd been roughly shaken and all her insides emptied on to the floor. But then she couldn't complain, she would hate him to keep secrets from her.

'Isabel, I think you could help us to catch the person who carried out these assaults.'

'Do you think it's the same man who's writing to me and sending me these ghastly "presents"?'

'Possibly.'

'Did he write letters to them? The women he attacked?'

'No, but he sent them locks of their own hair.'

'Oh no!' She closed her eyes. 'Does this get any worse?'

'No.'

'Is there something you haven't told me?'

'I've told you everything. I promise, Isabel.'

Her eyes flared. 'That lock of hair mailed to me – what have you found out about it?'

'We haven't got the results of the DNA tests yet. But, for what it's worth, the other samples matched the hair of the person it was sent to.'

'Horrible, horrible, horrible!'

'Yes.' He gave her a few moments to grow calmer. 'Will you help us find this person?' he asked quietly. 'Get him committed to trial, locked up?'

She looked at him and gave a slow inclination of her head. 'Yes, I will. What do you want me to do?'

'I think we know quite a lot about this man now. We know that he's attracted to redheads in the twenty-five to thirty age group. Single, independent women with responsible jobs. We know that he likes to tease and frighten them. And then he attacks.'

'Why am I getting letters when they didn't?'

'That's a very good question. My belief is that this man is becoming progressively more sophisticated with each of his targets. With the first victim, he simply mailed locks of hair. With the second, he sent locks of hair and then a pair of surgical scissors.' He stopped.

'Go on,' Isabel said.

He spread his hands. 'No, no, that's enough.'

'Is it that you don't want to upset me, or you can't tell me for some obscure legal reason? Which?'

He sighed. 'Both.'

'You'd better tell me,' she insisted fiercely. 'How can I work with you, trust you, if you don't me the whole truth?'

'Very well. Along with the scissors there was a recent photograph of his target.'

'Cut to shreds, I presume?'

'Yes.' He looked steadily at her. 'You're very astute,' he said.

'I've always had an active imagination, and it's come on in leaps and bounds since all this repulsive business started up,' she said grimly. 'OK, just tell me exactly what it is you want me to do.'

'I want you to place an advert in one or two lonely heart columns and try to flush him out. Meet him and trap him into incriminating himself.'

For a moment she was utterly baffled, the words wouldn't sink in. 'Good heavens,' she said quietly. 'I'd never have guessed at that, not in a million years.'

'Don't rule it out,' he urged her. 'I truly believe it's worth a try. The only thing the first two women had in common was that they both placed advertisements in the dating columns of newspapers. We think he responded to the ads, arranged to meet them, then stalked them.We could put our heads together and compose an advert, bearing in mind what we know of this man. You see, I suspect he's desperately lonely, the kind of person who probably takes several newspapers and spends time combing through them.'

'But if you know all this, why haven't you managed to track him down through the papers or the ads?'

'We think he must have used an alias, a false address and so on. The men the other women *could* identify have been ruled out – they all had solid alibis for the time of the attacks.' Max knew he was placing a terrible burden on the shoulders of this fragile young woman. 'Believe me Isabel, if there was any other way…'

'And what guarantee of safety do I have?' she cut in.

'We'll provide you with constant cover outside the flat. You'll have cover when you go out walking, an officer tracking you. And when you fix up a meeting with this man – which I suggest must only be in a cafe or restaurant of your choice – then I will be there personally to protect you.'

There was a long silence. 'Very well, then. I'll do it,' she told him. 'Anything is better than simply waiting for him to choose his moment to pounce.' She got up and took sheets of paper and a pen from her briefcase which she had dropped on the floor by the sofa when Max Hawthorne had brought her home from work that morning. Doing something active and positive to catch this tormentor of women had fired her resolve, sent her adrenaline pumping. 'Let's do it,' she said to Max. 'Compose the advert. Now! Strike while the iron's hot.'

'You're a very courageous woman,' he said, smiling and joining her at the table. She pushed the cartons and plates to one side and wrote 'Project – Ensnare the Villain' in bold letters at the top of the page. 'I don't know much about these sort of adverts,' she said, frowning. 'I've never really looked at them.'

'Don't worry, I'm an expert,' he said wryly.

'Are you?' She stared at him in dismay. Was he that desperate? Surely not.

'In my professional capacity,' he said with a slight twinkle in his eye.

'Ah.'

'I suggest we start with "Lively, fun-loving redhead seeks a companion with a view to a loving relationship..." Something along those lines.' He glanced across at her, sensing she was not listening, that she was preoccupied. 'Isabel?' he prompted.

'Are you married, Inspector?' she demanded impulsively, unable to stop herself.

'My wife died four years ago.' The muscles of his face tensed.

'Oh! I'm so sorry.'

'Yes.' His face was dark and closed. 'Shall we get on?'

'I don't like this,' she said sharply. 'You get to know all about me, but it seems I'm completely out of order if I ask a simple question about you. And another thing, you call me Isabel, but I still feel it would be presumptuous to call you Max. It's almost as though we were teacher and child, or the boss and his minion.'

'It's never been my intention that you should feel like that,' he said stiffly. 'Please feel free to call me Max.'

There was an awkward pause. 'Sorry,' she said. 'My emotions are all over the place at the moment. Take no notice, Max. Right, back to the advert.' She pursed her lips in thought. 'We know this monster likes long legs and big breasts – should we make something of that?'

She looked at him for a response. 'You're smiling,' she exclaimed. 'A proper smile.'

'It has been known before,' he said. 'And I think your suggestion is excellent. But we don't want our man to think you're a flirt or a tart. This bloke prefers quality. And he's got a thing about girls with auburn hair.'

'OK. How's this? "Leggy, curvaceous red-head, slim but not dim, seeks to lure gullible villain into her spider's web". Well..?'

'Getting closer. Now can we be serious?'

They spent the next half hour dreaming up words and phrases, juggling them around, ditching them, resurrecting them. In the end they came up with something spare and simple, but hopefully irresistible to the man they were seeking. 'Flame-haired career girl in her late twenties, seeks caring, sensitive man for companionship and stimulating conversation.'

They had argued about the word 'caring'. Isabel had

not thought it at all appropriate, but Max had argued that the man they were after most likely perceived himself in that way. After all. he was prepared to go to great lengths to devise ways to frighten his victims. 'Caring' in the sense of meticulous.

Replies were to be sent to a box number. Max would pick them up, then he and his team would sieve out likely candidates to discuss with Isabel. And she would then contact the chosen ones.

'We'll get you a new mobile phone, especially for this project,' Max told her. 'You'll be completely anonymous, untraceable.'

'Please God!' she whispered as she laid down her pen. Her surge of sparkling confidence and mischievous humour had suddenly fled. She knew that Max would soon leave her and there was another lonely, fearful night to get through. Even with a police car outside and an officer on watch, she still felt on edge and tense.

He slipped into his coat and turned up the collar. He turned to her at the door, his lips framing the words, 'Goodnight.'

'You're really worried about me, aren't you?' she asked softly before he could say the words.

'Yes.'

'Me as a person. Not just a victim?'

'Oh Isabel,' he sighed.

She felt his spirit reaching out to her fear and loneliness. She stretched out her left hand and straightened the left corner of his collar with a slow, lingering movement. Her hand stayed there, her fingers feeling the warmth of his neck.

She had a sensation of dissolving as his hands came around her face, his fingers slipping into her hair, cradling her skull as though it was infinitely precious. She heard a low moan, but was not sure if it was him or her. Then he was tracing her lips with his forefinger, very slowly, very tenderly. She closed her eyes. It was as though all the outlines of her body were liquifying, becoming misty and unsubstantial.

'Kiss me, Max,' she whispered, sinking against him, feeling the beats of his heart.

Slowly he bent his head to hers. He kissed her forehead and her eyebrows and her eyes, and then he kissed her mouth – at first tenderly, exploring. And then crushing his mouth against hers, as if their lips could merge, going beyond the barriers of skin and flesh. He held her as if they were both drowning and he must save her. He tasted her as if he were starving.

When she opened her eyes at last, he was looking down at her as though she were the loveliest thing he had ever seen.

She was trembling and exhausted. She wanted him never to leave her. She wanted to fall into a deep, deep sleep with his arms close around her. At the same time, though, she knew that he *had* to leave. That for him, the last few minutes should never have happened.

'You have to go,' she told him. 'Don't say anything. This was all my fault. Just go.'

It was not until he reached the top of the steps that she realised she had dismissed him very thoroughly.

chapter eight

Isabel woke early the next morning and rang to make an appointment at her doctor's surgery. She then rang for a taxi to take her there, and asked the driver to wait outside so that he could drive her on to the office.

Isabel had only visited the surgery once before when she had registered at the practice. She had never met the doctor who re-bandaged her hand, making it easier to be economical with the truth when he asked her how the injury had occurred. She told a little story about tidying out some drawers for her father, unexpectedly coming across one of his old razors. It could well have been true, apart from the fact that her father was miles away in Edinburgh. But the doctor was not to know that and he reported that the cuts were healing well. He put bandages on the two affected fingers only, and her hand instantly felt freed up and more normal.

Sitting in the taxi on the way to the office, she wondered why she should have this need to hide what was happening to her, to keep it a secret between her and the police.

She realised that there was a strange kind of shame in revealing yourself as the target of a perverted harasser. It was as though you had deliberately set out to attract the attention of some crazed person with dark and sleazy intentions, as though you were somehow a party to his evil desires. She felt she had read something of those thoughts in both Jack Cheney's and Emma Hayes's eyes. But not Max. He did not make her feel shamed or in any way 'tarnished'.

'Max', she whispered to herself, and just saying his name made her body grow warm with the memory of what had happened between them the night before. She tried not to think about it – she had work to do.

Once in her office, she rang through to the personal assistant of the senior partner who had frowned at her so suspiciously the previous morning and requested an urgent private meeting with him. There was some resistance due to about how busy he was, but Isabel's firm insistence eventually persuaded the PA to discover a window of opportunity at ten-fifteen that morning.

Isabel was smiling and outwardly confident as she entered the partner's room. He gave a cordial wave, inviting her to sit down in front of his vast, gleaming desk.

'I need to explain to you why the police came to see me at the office yesterday,' she told him.

'Oh, I'm sure there's a perfectly simple explanation,' he said graciously. 'Although I have to say that Inspector Hawthorne's attitude was pretty high-handed, demanding to see you without delay and so on.' He gave a faint smile. 'It's a very long time since anyone spoke to me in that authoritative way. I suppose I've got used to calling the shots myself for so long, I find it rather unnerving when someone turns the tables on me.'

His frankness was appealing and Isabel warmed to him. Almost to the point of telling him the whole truth...but still she held back.

'I can't give you the full details of my involvement with the police. For legal reasons,' she added, thinking that sounded a suitable excuse. 'But I'd like to assure you I'm not under suspicion for any criminal activities myself.'

'Good,' her boss said with a glinty look.

'I'm helping the police to try to catch someone who's assaulted two local women recently. They were doing house-to-house enquiries and when they got to me, they thought I'd be able to help.'

He traced a finger around the edge of his blotter. 'I hope you're not going to volunteer to do anything dangerous,' he remarked, making her realise how astute he was.

'No,' she agreed. 'Of course not. And my work will not be at all affected, I can totally assure you of that.'

'I'm delighted to hear it,' he smiled, although she was pretty sure she heard a hint of scepticism in his voice. 'Well, thank you for coming to share this information with me,' he said, standing up to indicate the interview was drawing to a close. 'And for being so frank. I appreciate that.'

Oh hell, thought Isabel walking back to her own office. She realised that her explanation had probably sounded pretty phoney. She should have either told the whole truth or a thumping and convincing lie. Damn. She'd made a mess of things. She had woken this morning determined to put this whole episode in perspective. She had wanted to prove to herself that she could do her work and keep her eye on the ball, despite this new hollow fear that had suddenly entered her life and now stalked it constantly. And probably all she had done was alert the senior partner to the fact that she was both vulnerable and evasive.

'Is it too early for coffee?' she asked Esther.

'It's never too early for coffee,' Esther assured her, switching on the machine. Today she was wearing a short chunky top in baby pink. It looked as though it had been knitted on hose-pipes. Her tiny skirt came to a point at the front and had a three inch black fringe attached to the hem.

Isabel smiled. 'You're looking good this morning,' she

told Esther, going through to her office and sitting down behind the desk. She set her computer to boot up and then started sorting through the morning mail. An image of Max Hawthorne's face got in the way. She started reliving the sensations his touch had aroused. She closed her eyes as though she could shut him out, but her heart was thudding beneath her blouse and her cheeks were suddenly burning. She felt jittery and fragile, as though she might shatter if someone said the slightest little thing to her.

The morning passed. She went to a managerial meeting with the administration department, as a new computer system was being set up throughout the company. It was vital for managers to understand the implications of the new technology, but she could hardly concentrate on a word. She made no contribution at all apart from spilling a jug of water on the table when she attempted to fill her glass. Eyes gazed at her curiously.

At one o'clock she telephoned the clinic where Luisa was to have her abortion. A crisp, polite voice told her that her sister was currently in theatre. She would be back in her room in another half-hour and Isabel was very welcome to visit any time after mid-afternoon.

'I'll come as soon as I can. Will you tell her that please?' Isabel responded, equally polite and crisp.

Esther went out and brought her back a warmed croissant filled with seafood. Isabel forced herself to eat every scrap, chewing each mouthful slowly and thoroughly. She recalled reading somewhere that oily fish was very good for the thinking parts of the brain. And Boy, do I need it? she thought grimly.

She willed herself to find some new energy. She read through her emails, which had mounted up to almost sixty because of her absence the day before. Then she made around ten phone calls, keeping each one very business-like, permitting no small talk. She sent some messages to individual members of her team and then she went through all the papers on her desk and dealt with them.

'Gosh, I can't keep up with you,' Esther exclaimed laughing when she saw the stack of papers to file.

'Have to make up for the lost time yesterday,' Isabel said, trying to ignore the waves of exhaustion which were now sweeping through her.

'How's your hand?' Esther asked.

'Much better.'

Esther looked at her for a long, thoughtful moment. 'That's good then,' she said, grasping the files and shimmying away on her four-inch wedge heels.

Just before five o'clock, Max called her on her mobile. 'We've placed the ads,' he told her tersely without any friendly preliminaries. 'Two of the free local papers and three of the nationals, tomorrow morning.'

'Right.' His voice was so clinical, so cool it seemed to gouge a hole inside her.

'And we have the DNA results from the hair samples. The lock you were sent and the strands you pulled out yourself. They match.'

She suddenly felt icy cold. 'No! I can't believe it.'

'I'm afraid so.' There was tiny beating pause. 'Isabel,' his voice was warm and urgent now, 'I do realise how upsetting all this is for you. I would completely understand if you wanted to change your mind about what we planned. It's quite in order to back out if you feel you can't take the strain. Just say.'

'Why should I back out? This man has dropped me into a horrible dark pit and I can't wait to get him behind bars.'

She bit hard on her lip, the inside of her skull feeling as though it would burst apart with rage at the thought of her tormentor. A man who had already battered two other harmless females. 'In fact, if he turns up, I think he'll be the one who needs protection, not me.'

'Isabel, are you all right?' His voice sounded worried now.

'Yes,' she snapped. 'I know I sound like a mad woman, but there's something about all this harassment that makes ordinary polite hedging seem like a total waste of time.'

'Yes, I see,' he said carefully. He was back to formal, cautious Inspector mode. Well, he would be wouldn't he? She had basically given him the brush-off when she'd packed him off the previous evening.

'And for what it's worth, Max,' she continued, 'when you kissed me last night, it was the best thing that's happened to me for a very long time. So don't waste a second of your time feeling guilty.'

She pushed the button to end the call. The phone rang again almost immediately, but she ignored it.

She left the office early and took a taxi to the clinic where Luisa was recovering from her operation. She remembered that Max had suggested that public transport was the safest way to travel, and she agreed. But trying to get to Luisa's clinic from Central London on either the tube or the bus would take double the time, and she couldn't bear to spend all that time crushed amongst a crowd of strangers. After all, the monster could be travelling with her for all she knew! She judged that a taxi was fairly safe as long as she hailed one on the street, and one from which another passenger was alighting.

The clinic was warm and hushed and smelled of freesias and lilies. Walking to Luisa's room, Isabel was guiltily conscious of coming along empty-handed. She simply hadn't thought about gifts of flowers or fruit. Just keeping on top of the normal details of life seemed to be becoming increasingly hard.

Luisa was sitting in bed, wearing a gorgeous 1930's style apricot silk dressing gown embroidered with burgundy dragons. A man sat beside the bed. He was young, with lovely facial bones, soft brown eyes and a mass of thick blond hair. A man she hadn't met before. She realised it must be Josh.

He stood up and smiled, putting out a hand to greet her. 'Hi, I'm Josh. You're Isabel. Luisa's told me all about you.'

Not all, Isabel thought with grim irony, feeling that she was now a rather different person from the woman she had been as recently as two weeks ago...before the monster entered her life. Before Max Hawthorne arrived on the scene, a man to make her pulses jump and stretch the strings of her heart to breaking point. 'Hello Josh,' she said brightly, shaking his hand.

She turned to Luisa who was looking pale, but very beautiful. 'How are you?' she murmured, bending to kiss her.

'I'm fine. It all went perfectly. They pumped me full of pain-killers when I came round. And Josh was there when they wheeled me back. Wasn't that absolutely sweet?' She turned to Josh and gazed at him adoringly.

Totally amazing, was Isabel's private thought. She knew that some modern men were very relaxed and tolerant on sexual matters. But to visit your new lover when she'd just aborted the baby of another man did seem remarkably enlightened. Watching Josh watch Luisa, as time went by she got the impression he was simply infatuated, that it wouldn't matter to him what Luisa did.

Luisa had always had this ability to fascinate men. There was something fiercely female, yet desperately vulnerable, about her that made them beat a path to her door. The problem was, thought Isabel, her heart sinking slightly, that the more intense the infatuations, the sooner they seemed to dissolve into thin air. And then Luisa was left bereft and prone to frightening, black episodes of depression. Oh well, at least Josh had a lovely, warm, genuine smile, thought Isabel. A kind of innocent cherub look. Maybe, just maybe, this time it would be different.

'Hey!' Josh said after a while, spotting Isabel's bandages. 'What have you done to your hand?'

'Oh, I just got caught up with the food processor blades,' Isabel responded swiftly.

'Ugh, nasty!' Josh gave a little shudder, his eyes wide with sympathy. 'Listen,' he said getting to his feet, 'I'll make myself scarce and go flirt with the nurses and get them to feed me tea and buns.' He winked at Luisa and then at Isabel. 'Give you two girls time to have a gossip. Or whatever it is girls do together.'

Luisa's eyes followed him as he left the room. She had a worryingly besotted expression.

'He's nice,' Isabel said, thinking that sounded rather lame. 'Lovely sweet smile.'

'Yeah. He's a peach.' Luisa put her head on one side and viewed Isabel with a look of growing concern. 'Sweetie, you've got the most dreadful dark rings under your eyes. Have you been working too hard?'

'It's a busy time in the financial year,' Isabel said lightly. 'Coming up to the end of the tax year and so on.'

Luisa turned away slightly. She took a sip of the water on her bedside locker. 'I worry about you,' she said suddenly.

'I'm fine. Come on, it's not like you to be a mother-hen type.' She stopped. 'Oh Heavens, that was crass and clumsy.'

'It's OK. You're quite right. I suppose I'm just feeling sentimental and sisterly.'

'It's probably the anaesthetic,' Isabel said, wrapping her arms around Luisa. 'Actually, there is something I'm worried about.' At least now she was telling the genuine truth.

'Yes?'

'Father. I got a letter from him yesterday. His writing is looking a bit shaky. I keep forgetting he's quite an old man now, so I thought I might go up and see him at the weekend.' Oh God, she thought. How am I going to do that with the police on my tail? What will Max say if I leave London? Will it interfere with the 'plan'? She decided she would go anyway. Why should the monster rule her life? Or Max, for that matter?

'He'll be perfectly all right,' Luisa said, her face suddenly hard. 'You know Father. He's as strong as the proverbial ox. He'll outlive us both most likely.'

'Well, much as I love him, I don't want to die young,' Isabel said quietly, a shiver running through her.

'Sorry, Izzie. It was just a figure of speech. You know how bad things have been between me and Father in recent years. We just seem to rub each other up the wrong way.' She sighed as her fingers kneaded the crisp white sheet covering her stomach. 'I'm afraid I've been a dreadful disappointment to him.'

'I won't mention anything to him about the abortion,' Isabel reassured her.

Isabel grimaced. 'No. You're one hundred percent trustworthy, darling. Lucky he's got one daughter with a touch of moral fibre.'

'Stop putting yourself down,' Isabel told her softly. Luisa's words had triggered a prick of conscience. She felt uneasy, as though she were deceiving Luisa by keeping silent about the unknown man who was threatening her and the fear that was constantly stalking her. For a moment she was tempted to share those fears with her sister, but when she looked at Luisa's drawn, tired face, she changed her mind.

Josh reappeared. 'Hey, you two look as though you need a bit of cheering up,' he said, sensing the atmosphere. He perched on the edge of the bed and began to regale them with stories of designing and building stage sets in London and Sydney and New York, squeezing the last drop of humour out of the tales of things that had gone wrong. On one occasion, a piece of scenery had fallen down on the first night, revealing two famous male actors in a clinch backstage! As he talked, he used his delicate sensitive hands to illustrate his points. Both Luisa and Isabel felt themselves pulled out of their low mood.

He's good for her, Isabel thought, as she left the two of them together and walked out of the clinic into the street on the look-out for a taxi. As the cab threaded through the traffic towards her flat, she remembered Josh's boyish grin and his twinkling eyes. Yes, maybe he was just what Luisa needed at the moment. A young man to care for and indulge.

The taxi driver parked the cab and Isabel jumped out and paid the fare. 'There's a police car outside your place, love,' the driver commented dryly. 'Hope you're not in bother!'

'You'd be surprised!' Isabel responded with irony.

Giving a brief glance at the police car, and thinking how

odd it was to have someone constantly keeping a watch on you, she ran down the steps, key at the ready and let herself into the flat.

Two minutes later, as she was scrambling eggs for supper and pouring herself a glass of wine, the door buzzer sounded. Three short blasts. Isabel stood very still, her body tensed. Even with the police car outside, she still felt a rush of fear when there was someone at the door. She walked into the hallway and stood looking worriedly at the door as it had a life of its own.

'Who is it?' she called out.

'It's me love, Flo.'

Isabel gave a sigh of relief and opened the door. 'Come on in Flo.'

'I won't stop a minute, love,' Flo said, stepping inside and looking around her at the pale paintwork and the Japanese-style lamps. 'Oh, your place is so smart, Isabel. So stylish. It puts mine to shame.'

'Not at all,' Isabel said gallantly. 'Will you have some sherry?'

'Just a little one.' Flo sat down and Isabel went to find the sweet sherry she kept especially for Flo's occasional visits. 'You haven't been to see me for a few days,' Flo remarked, as Isabel handed her a glass. 'I was wondering if you were all right, love.'

Isabel winced with fresh guilt. 'I'm so sorry, Flo. I've been caught up with…so many things. Oh dear!'

'You don't need to apologise, love. I knew it would be like that. I just got a bit worried about you, that's all.'

'You are sweet. But there's no need to worry, I'm fine. How are things with you? Any more…visits?'

'All quiet on the Western Front,' said Flo with a grin. 'Not a murmur. You must have scared them off good and proper.'

'Excellent! Hope it stays that way.'

'Listen, I've got some news,' Flo announced with an air of triumph. 'I'm going to stay with my sister in Cambridge for two weeks. We'll be out-and-about in the town shopping and off to the theatre and wine bars, and goodness knows what. She's got it all arranged. And what do you think of this, I've booked a seat on the train. Travelling by myself, totally independent.'

'That's great, Flo. I'm really pleased for you. It's ages since you've been anywhere isn't it?'

'I've been a real little stop-at-home,' Flo agreed. 'So I've come to ask if you'll keep an eye on the flat while I'm away.'

'Of course I will.'

'You know, Isabel, I feel it's changed my life for me, those kids not coming around, taunting me any more. It'd really had been bothering me. My sister's been saying to me for ages, "Come and stay, Flo. We'll have a little holiday together..." And I've been saying, "No, no, no–" because I felt such a useless old thing, scared and hiding away all the time. And now, somehow, I feel quite different. And I'm saying "Yes, yes, yes." Isn't it strange?'

'It makes perfect sense to me,' Isabel said slowly. 'Not strange at all. I'm so pleased for you Flo.'

'Well, it's all down to you, love. I couldn't have faced them in a hundred years. They wouldn't have taken a scrap of notice of me.'

Flo was persuaded to have a second sherry and Isabel sat back and listened to the now-familiar tales of Flo's past. She put a smile of interest on her face, but her thoughts had inevitably gone back to the man out there who wanted to do her harm. The man she and Max were going to catch.

After Flo had left, Isabel ate her supper, rinsed the dishes in the sink and tidied the kitchen. The time moved on to ten o'clock.

She took a long soak in a scented bath and slipped into a towelling robe. She switched on the TV, flicking through the channels, knowing that she was simply putting off the time when she would go to bed and lie staring up into the darkness.

Just before eleven, the buzzer sounded again, sending jabs of anxiety through Isabel's nerves. Her mouth dry, she went to stand behind the door.

'Who is it?' she asked sharply.

'Max,' came the reply. His voice was unmistakable, deep and full.

She swung open the door and he walked straight in. He stood looking down at her. 'I'm not on duty,' he said.

Isabel felt as though a great weight had rolled away from her as she closed her eye and tilted her face up. He pulled her into his arms.

chapter nine

He kissed her until she ached with longing. Long, long moments passed by and they were still standing behind the front door. She drew away from him a little and gazing up into his eyes, she took his hand and led him into her bedroom.

She had switched on the lamps earlier and the room was filled with soft light glowing from the apricot silk shades. Still gazing into his face, she put her arms up around his neck.

'Does this feel right?' he asked slowly.

'Perfect,' she whispered.

He loosened her arms from his neck and placed them gently by her sides. Then he put his hands on her shoulders and turned her body away from him. Very slowly he began to massage the base of her neck. His fingers were both strong and gentle as he moved his hands over her shoulders and the tops of her arms, easing away all the strain and dread of the past days and weeks. She felt his thumbs trace rhythmic circles along her shoulder blades. His fingers crept up to her hairline, healing fingers driving the tension from the hollows below her skull.

Her eyelids drooped in pleasure as his hands dropped to the small of her back, his thumbs moving up her spine, easing the rigid muscles into relaxation. She felt as though she would melt.

But now she wanted something else from him. She turned in his arms and lifted her face for another kiss. He wrapped her in his arms with fierce urgency and she could feel the heat of his body and its spare, lean tautness. Her nipples hardened under her robe as he kissed her again, a long, long kiss that sent stabs of desire racing through her body. As his hand slipped inside her robe and his fingers danced light as air over her skin, electric shivers flew up her backbone and darted across the top of her skull.

She arched against his chest and kissed him back hard, her mouth moving to match the rhythm of his breathing.

He undid the tie of her robe and slipped it down over her shoulders. She stood naked in front of him, trembling slightly with apprehension and anticipation.

'Isabel,' he said in a kind of groan, 'Dear God, you're so very lovely.'

Isabel helped him off with his jacket and unbuttoned his shirt. His arms were strong and muscled, the skin tight and smooth. She smiled up into his beautiful warrior face and then she bent and untied his shoes and when he had stepped out of them, she unzipped his jeans and eased them slowly down over his hips and buttocks. His stomach was firm and flat, with a line of dark hair running down it.

Soon, he too was naked. He lifted a hand and, very gently, pushed a strand of stray hair behind her ear. Then he lifted her into his arms and laid her on the bed.

They held each other as if they would never let go. They tasted each other's skin; he kissed her face all over and ran his lips across her ear.

'My love,' Isabel murmured, 'my wonderful Max.'

He smiled at her, then placed his hands on her hips and pulled her against him. She could feel his hardness and she kissed him again. His leg pressed between her thighs, and she felt an explosion of sensation as his hand gently caressed her, his stroke light as a cobweb. She arched her back and moaned as his touch obliterated everything except his nearness and the exquisite sensation of his entering her body and moving inside her.

Afterwards he lay beside her, brushing her warm damp hair from her face, then touching her lips with his finger.

'What are you thinking?' she asked softly, running her fingers through his soft, thick hair. 'Talk to me Max. Say something to me.'

She trembled inwardly, fearing he was already regretting the wonderful communication they had shared.

He didn't respond immediately. Instead he took the cover away from her body and gently ran his fingers down her neck, and between her breasts and over her stomach. Isabel shivered. He bent and kissed each breast.

'I was thinking,' he said, 'that I would like to keep you very close to me – forever.' Wonderful words, but he spoke them with soft regret as though he did not believe they would come true. 'What are *you* thinking?'

'The same,' she said. 'I'm thinking that we are probably both completely mad, and I'm not at all sure you should be here. And – I'm thinking that I don't know anything about you Max,' she said with a wistful smile. 'Except that you've just made me very, very happy indeed.'

He didn't smile back. He looked at her tenderly, but with a deep seriousness she found faintly unsettling. 'What do you want to know?'

'Everything.' She ran her fingers over his chest. 'Well, maybe not all at once.'

'All right then, where do you want to start?' There was still no smile.

She leaned up on one elbow. 'Tell me about your wife.'

There was a long silence and she felt herself blush. 'I'm sorry, I shouldn't have asked that.'

'Her name was Jennifer. We'd been married four years when she became pregnant. She was over the moon. And then, ten weeks before the baby was due, she had an emergency Caesarean,' he said in a low, flat voice. 'The baby died. And then Jenny got an abscess in the wound under the stitches. The medics went into overdrive to combat the infection but she died three days later.'

Isabel took his hand in hers. 'Oh, Max.'

'She'd wanted the baby so much – we both had. It was a little girl. Ten weeks premature.'

They lay together in silence for a time. 'I'd always thought of myself as a happy person before that,' he told her. 'I had an idyllic childhood, loving parents, a sister to spar with. I did well at school. I took a degree in criminal law, thinking I'd probably read for the bar. But I was attracted to a more dangerous life, so I joined the police force.'

'And you didn't regret it?'

'Not at all. And since Jenny died, it's been my salvation, my life.'

Isabel gave herself time to think over all he had said. 'You've taken a huge risk coming here to be with me, haven't you?' she asked slowly.

'Getting involved with the people whose cases you're working on is a total "no-go" area.' His grey eyes were hard as he turned to face her.

'What would happen if it came to light?' she asked, her alarm for him tightening her throat muscles.

'I'd be disciplined. Probably suspended.'

'Dismissed from the force?'

'It's possible.'

She leaned close to him and kissed his lips. A long, deep, loving kiss. An expression of her utter belief in him. A token of how much his wayward passion had meant to her. *Did* mean to her, she corrected herself hastily. 'You mustn't come here again, Max. Not – like this. We must find somewhere else to be together.'

He said nothing. Maybe there won't be another time, she thought in panic, looking at his stripped, emotionless features. 'How did you get past the officers on watch outside?' she wondered curiously.

'I told them I'd take over. Gave them the night off!'

'Oh God, Max, wasn't that risky?'

'Yes.'

'You'll have to be sure to be back in your car before the next watch comes along.'

'Yes.' A slow smile illuminated his face. 'Don't worry, I'll be there.'

She lay beside him, miserably guilty that she had been a party to his putting his career on the line.

'Isabel,' he said tenderly. 'I'm not regretting what's happened between us tonight. I'm glad. I'd do it all over again. Do you believe that?'

She put her hands in a protecting cradle around his face. 'Of course. You've no need to persuade me with words, my love. You're here. That says everything.'

With his arms around her, she sank into a deep well of sleep for the first time in weeks. When she woke, he had already left.

chapter ten

Isabel stood at the window of her office looking down into the street below. Her eyes vaguely registered the steadily moving procession of pedestrians on the pavements either side of the road and the solid jam of traffic between. It was two days since she and Max had made love. Two whole days since she had seen him, and it seemed like a lonely eternity. He had sent red roses to the office the day before. A huge bunch wrapped in crackling cellophane lined with soft, gilded tissue. The message on the accompanying card simply said 'M'. Her heart had twisted when she saw it and she had been touched and yet strangely saddened, wondering if she and Max had any realistic hope of a future together. Somehow the memory of their love-making seemed dreamlike and unreal. Even the roses seemed improbable; she couldn't imagine Max standing grimly in the florists ordering such a bold and sentimental bouquet.

He had telephoned once, enquiring about her well-being. He had sounded tense and formal and, whilst the words he had spoken had been caring and considerate, there was no emotion she could hear in his voice except caution and restraint.

She sat down at her desk and forced herself to concentrate on the papers Esther had laid out for her attention. After an hour had gone by, she straightened up in her chair, moving and rotating her shoulders in an attempt to rid herself of the tension she could feel there. She recalled

Max's fingers moving over her tensed muscles, and let out a soft, groaning sigh.

Her mobile phone lay on the desk and she kept staring at it, willing it to ring. She so wanted Max to call her again, and found herself longing just to hear his voice. But the phone remained stubbornly silent. It was like a form of torture. Impulsively, she snatched the phone up and punched in her father's number in Edinburgh.

It rang and rang and she became anxious. She wished her father would make use of an answering service but he disdained what he called 'new fangled technology' – mobile phones, computers, and so forth. Just as she was giving up hope of contacting him, his voice came on the line; precise and clipped, each syllable perfectly articulated as he carefully recited his full name and his phone number.

'Isabel, my dear!' he exclaimed on hearing her voice. 'This isn't your normal time of day to telephone me. Should you not be working in your office at this time of the day?'

'I am at the office, Father. But I do occasionally have a minute for private matters.' Isabel smiled, knowing her father's concern for diligence and correctness where 'matters of business' as he called them, were concerned.

'Indeed. Well, I suppose you do. Of course it was not like that in my young days.'

'No, of course. I simply phoned to ask how you are, I shan't be wasting any business time.'

'I'm well, my dear.' There was a pause. 'Yes, I'm quite well, indeed I am.' He cleared his throat, a harsh, gruff sound.

Isabel was instantly alarmed. He never ever qualified his robust statements about his good health. 'What do you mean by "quite well"? Is there a problem.'

'Noo,' he said dismissively, spinning the word out, making his Scottish accent more noticeable than usual.

'Are you sure?' Isabel gripped the phone tightly. 'Father, you must tell me if there's anything wrong. It wouldn't be fair to keep things from me.'

'Just a slight problem with my heart,' he said dismissively. 'It's nothing for you to get worried about.'

Oh God! She could hear now in his voice that all was not well; a slight breathlessness, a tiny faltering in his normally-immaculate delivery of speech. 'How long has this been going on? Have you seen the doctor? Are you having treatment?'

'The doctor has been to pay me a visit a couple of times this week. Just to check me over, you know. She's a nice wee girl, but I rather fancy she's wasting her time.'

'What do you mean?'

'Well, nature takes its course when you get to my age, my dear. No use arguing with it.'

'I'm coming up to see you,' Isabel said firmly. 'This weekend.'

'There's no need, my dear. I shall be perfectly fine. Mrs Pringle looks after all my needs.'

'Mrs Pringle is your housekeeper,' Isabel protested. 'She may cook your meals and keep the house clean and tidy, but she can't care for you like a daughter.'

'There is no denying that, Isabel, bearing-in-mind that she is nearly as old as me,' he said drily. 'No, my dear, I don't want you dashing up here when you have your job and your life in London to think about.'

'I'm coming,' she said. 'And that's that. I'll get the five o'clock train from King's Cross.'

'No, dear,' he repeated very firmly. 'I'd prefer it if you did not.'

'But why?'

There was a tiny pause. 'Because I shan't be here.'

Isabel felt a swooping sensation in her stomach. 'Father, what do mean by that?'

'I'm due to go into hospital on Friday. Just for observation, a few routine tests. Nothing at all to get bothered about.'

'Oh my God!' she exclaimed. 'I'm most definitely coming.'

'No Isabel,' he warned sharply. 'Please listen to me. I don't want you to come, I mean it.'

'Oh, Good Heavens!' she exclaimed, hurt. 'Why not?'

'Because it will make me feel as though I'm at death's door if you drop everything to rush to my bedside. Will you please stay put in London, my dear, and enjoy yourself this weekend. There'll be time enough to come and see me when I'm home again, up and about, properly dressed and with my dignity back in place. Please humour me on this point.'

She knew there was nothing to be gained from further protests. Her father had always been hugely proud and impossibly stubborn. She laid her phone down on the desk and sat still for a moment, thinking over the conversation.

Esther came in with freshly-made coffee. She looked worriedly at Isabel's white face. 'Bad news?' she asked.

Isabel made herself smile. It struck her she must be getting to be something of a liability for her sensitive, observant assistant.

'I've just been speaking to my father,' she explained. 'He tells me he has some kind of heart problem. But he wouldn't say how serious.'

'Oh, poor you,' said Esther. 'First that horrid accident with your hand and now this.'

'Mmm,' smiled Isabel, regretfully thinking that those were not the only issues that were troubling her.

'Oh!,' said Esther, turning back at the door, 'an Inspector Hawthorne called while you were speaking to your father. He wants you to call him back. It sounded urgent.'

Isabel nodded and reached for her phone. Max answered instantly.

There were no loving preliminaries. This was clearly a business call from the office, she could hear the murmur of voices and phones ringing in the background. 'There's been a good response to the adverts,' he told her crisply. 'We've been through the replies very carefully and picked four men who seem promising in matching up with our suspect.'

'Good,' Isabel said with a weary sigh. She was beginning to wonder if she could go through with Max's plan. It was not the risk element that bothered her most, as she trusted Max to have excellent safety precautions in place for her meetings with the various men. It was her own capability for acting and deception that worried her, especially when there was so much at stake. Although she was very competent at her job, she had never considered herself an especially extroverted person. In fact, when in company with strange men in a social setting, she had always felt a certain reserve and shyness.

'Are you having second thoughts?' he asked evenly.

'No. No! I'll do it. We need to get this man. Not just for my sake, but for all those other poor women out there he might fixate on and turn their lives into a nightmare.'

'Thank you,' he said gently. 'We appreciate that.'

'We?'

'My team. And, of course, myself.'

'So, when is it going to happen? These meetings you're setting up?'

'As soon as possible. Maybe not tomorrow, but the evening after that. And then, hopefully, the next three evenings.'

'Oh.'

'Is there a problem?' he asked, and she had a mental image of his eyes sharpening with conjecture.

'My father's ill, I had been thinking of going to Edinburgh this weekend to see him.'

'Oh dear,' he said. 'I'm sorry.'

'That my father is ill or that I'm going to Edinburgh?'

'That your father is ill, of course.'

'He's absolutely adamant I shouldn't rush off to be with him,' she told Max. 'It's a question of pride. He doesn't want to admit that he's not in the rudest of health. And he most certainly doesn't want me to see him in his pyjamas.' Tears came into her eyes when she thought of her fastidious, ferociously-independent father and the prospect of him losing a grip on his health and self-respect. But why was she telling Max all this? And in such fierce tones, as if it were all his fault.

'Do you want to go?' Max asked her calmly, but she could hear a note of concern in his voice. If she were to go to Edinburgh on Friday, it would certainly scupper his plans to try to flush out the harasser without delay.

'Yes,' she told him, 'but he says I mustn't. It's something of a dilemma.'

'It is,' Max agreed quietly.

'What would you do if I said I was going?' she asked with a touch of challenge. 'Would you try to stop me? I realise it would spoil your plans for going ahead with these "dates" you want to arrange, and you'd be worried about my safety as well, but if I want to go then that's my decision. Isn't it?' For Heaven's sake, stop babbling, she told herself.

'Yes,' he said patiently. 'So, do you intend to travel to Edinburgh at the weekend?'

'I don't know.' She felt pushed into a corner, frustrated and childishly mulish. 'But if I do decide to go, then that's my affair.'

'Of course it is. Your father's well-being must come first. But it would be helpful for you to let us know what you decide as soon as you can,' he said with quiet reasonableness.

'Yes,' she agreed, miserable with indecision.

'Shall we go ahead on the assumption that you'll be here in London at the weekend, Isabel? For the present, at least. The team need something positive to work on.' His voice had a certain steeliness that warned her not to put up any more obstacles.

'Very well.'

'Sergeant Hayes and I would like to see you as soon as possible to discuss setting up the meetings with the four men we've selected. Might we call at your home this evening. Say around seven?'

Isabel felt light and disoriented. She recalled being in bed with Max two evenings before, the way her body had opened up to him. And here he was now talking to her with such distant politeness, as though she were a mere acquaintance. She recalled how much she had learned about passion in that one evening making love with him. Max had released feelings which had astonished her, making her gasp and melt at his touch. She remembered how his body had crushed her, hard and tough against her feminine softness. How her nipples had burned between his lips.

A slow, rising warmth washed through her as she stood in her office, a quiet workaday creature in a sleek, charcoal-grey suit.

'Yes,' she said faintly. 'Around seven will be fine.'

They arrived exactly on the hour. Emma Hayes stepped inside first. She was wearing uniform which made her look sterner than ever. Isabel wondered if she had put it on as a deliberate ploy to emphasise the seriousness of the mission they were about to embark on.

Max sat in corner of the sofa, his long legs stretched out in front of him, his face calm and inscrutable. Isabel hardly dare look at him, afraid that her feelings would spill out from her eyes, shrieking out a damning message to the rigidly-correct Sergeant Hayes.

Emma took the lead in presenting the brief biographies written by the four men who had been selected for Isabel to meet, and in outlining the plan of action for the assignations. Isabel had the impression that Emma was nervous, that she was undergoing some kind of test with Max looking on as her evaluator and examiner. She felt a rush of sympathy for the ambitious young officer, pinned under Max's cool gaze.

'We've tried to match what we know about "The Batterer"...' Emma stopped suddenly, glancing uneasily at Max, whose only response was a slight raise of the eyebrows and a clear directive to Emma to fight her own battles. 'We call our suspect "The Batterer", Miss Bruce,' she explained to Isabel, two spots of pink appearing in her cheeks. 'It's a kind of code we use. I hope it doesn't upset you.'

'To know I'm going on a blind date with a man nicknamed The Batterer. No, not at all, Sergeant Hayes,' smiled Isabel with wicked irony, suddenly seeing the black humour within this deadly serious situation.

Emma Hayes cleared her throat nervously. 'The four men we've chosen for you to meet have all referred to the fact that they admire red-heads and women with high profile jobs. Or perhaps I should have put the jobs first,' she added, frowning.

'I think you were quite right to mention his liking of red-heads as the first important factor,' Isabel told the Sergeant. 'After all, he did send locks of hair to at least three women we know. So clearly hair is some kind of trigger for him. A sexual trigger, because, as we all know, this harassment he's carrying out is about sex, isn't it?'

Emma looked at her with new respect. 'Yes, that's exactly what we believe.'

Isabel glanced at Max, almost with defiance. His eyes linked with hers and she knew with a flash of pure animal sensation that he was her only love. The one true passion of her life, whatever should happen in the future. Whoever else might come along, if fate conspired against them, if they were forced to part.

'So how do you want me to play these meetings?' Isabel asked, curious to find herself suddenly strong and decisive after all the fear and uncertainty that had recently overwhelmed her. 'I've got to be a superb actress, haven't I? So what's the role you want me to play? The slick professional city woman, the seductress, the girl with a heart of gold? Or maybe all three?'

'Or maybe just yourself,' Max interposed softly. For Isabel, the low velvet of his voice was like a caress. She shot a swift glance at Emma Hayes, but the Sergeant's face wore its usual severe expression. She appeared not to have noticed anything unusual.

'We think it best for you simply to act as you would normally,' Sergeant Hayes confirmed.

'Maybe that's the hardest thing of all,' Isabel reflected. 'Putting on an act to be yourself. Especially as I personally would find it quite alarming to go on a blind date with someone I had advertised for.'

'Allowing yourself to appear uncertain and vulnerable is probably the most effective device you could use,' Max observed. 'It's quite normal to feel nervous on a blind date. And this man is very likely to be someone who feels socially inadequate and is highly aroused by being made to feel more powerful and confident than his companion.'

'I suppose that links up with his wanting to taunt his targets and frighten them. Control them, in fact,' Isabel reflected.

'We need you to put him at ease,' Sergeant Hayes said briskly. 'Get him in the mood to give away secrets about himself.'

Isabel nodded.

'We suggest the best way to do this is…' The Sergeant stopped abruptly, mindful that Max had put up his hand to indicate that Isabel should be allowed to speak.

'I think the way to tempt people to give away secrets is to tell them some of your own,' Isabel said reflectively.

Max smiled. 'Exactly.' He had been watching Isabel carefully, his eyes assessing and reflective. 'Are you still sure you want to go ahead?' he asked, giving her one of his unnervingly steady looks.

'Yes,' she said slowly. 'When can I see the letters these men wrote in response to the advert?'

'Now. I have them here.' Max reached into the inner pocket of his jacket. 'Ah!' he exclaimed with annoyance. 'They must be in my document case in the car.' He glanced at Emma Hayes who jumped up instantly. 'I'll get them, Sir.'

The door closed behind her and Isabel and Max stared at each other. 'Smart move,' Isabel whispered, her lips twitching with a smile. Slow and dreamlike they both stood up and moved towards each other. His arms went around her and their kiss was long and deep and rapturous.

'I am *aching* for you,' he murmured. He rubbed his hands over the muscles of her back and shoulders. 'The tension is still there. Oh God, my poor darling.'

'Is it any wonder?' she smiled wistfully. 'A madman's out to get me, my father is probably dangerously ill, and two nights ago I jumped into bed and fell in love with a man I hardly know.'

He looked deep into her eyes and kissed her again. Already they could hear Sergeant Hayes' tapping on the door to be let back in. Reluctantly they moved apart. 'Sit down,' Isabel mouthed to Max. 'We mustn't take any risks. It's too dangerous for you. I'm sure your Sergeant suspects something.'

She felt as though her lips were on fire with Max's kisses as she opened the door to Emma Hayes and she felt sure the other woman could feel the heat from her body, could sense the passion stalking the atmosphere.

But the Sergeant seemed oblivious. At a nod from Max, she took the letters from his case and handed them to Isabel who scanned them swiftly. She looked up, frowning.

'But these letters are so…ordinary. So formal and polite.' Surely the monster couldn't have penned anything as innocent-sounding as these brief notes.

'Quite,' Max agreed. 'But a woman like you wouldn't

have responded to anything flamboyant and over-familiar, would she?'

Isabel saw the sense in that.

'We believe this man is clever,' Max observed. 'Maybe highly-educated. He's canny enough not to frighten his victims off.'

'OK, I'll buy that,' Isabel said.

'Would you like to rank the letters in order?' Sergeant Hayes suggested. 'Choose the person you think you would like to meet first?'

'I don't think I'd like to meet any of them if I had the choice,' Isabel commented wryly. She sifted through the letters, swiftly putting them in order. She chose the shortest note first. It said simply:

'*Dear Red-haired lady,*

I am thirty-four years old and work as a management consultant. I would be most honoured to meet you if you would care to contact me.'

The letter had a stylish but illegible signature, and there was a contact number.

Max took a tiny, slender mobile phone from his case and handed it to her. 'This will ensure you have complete anonymity,' he said quietly. 'The Sergeant and I are going to leave now. When you've made contact with this first suspect and made an arrangement to meet, I'd like you to let me or one of the team know straight away.'

His eyes were as grey as a stormy sea, distant and entirely business-like.

Isabel looked at Max, her own eyes wide and haunted. Suddenly this venture which had seemed some kind of fantasy, had become horribly real. It was as though she had been standing shivering on a high diving board and now, finally, she knew she had no choice but to plunge headfirst into the water beneath.

Max slid his keys into the ignition and reached for his seat belt.

'Isabel Bruce has got guts, I'll give her that,' said Emma. 'Not many women outside the force would be prepared to put themselves on the line as she's doing.'

'No,' Max agreed, tense with apprehension on Isabel's behalf.

'It's lucky for us she's not attached or married,' Emma continued in her level, emotionless voice. 'I don't think the average husband would be too keen to let his wife turn up to blind dates…even with the police standing by.' She paused. 'And, incidentally, don't you think it's odd she's not attached, sir? An attractive woman like that?'

'Human life and love are full of puzzles, Emma,' Max observed slowly, shooting a thoughtful glance at his Sergeant, and warning himself to be very, very careful.

chapter eleven

When Isabel got into work the next day, Esther came hurrying into her office to tell her that one of the senior partners wanted to see her right away.

'Oh dear. Which of the partners? Is there a problem?' Isabel asked.

'Gareth Brown. You know – the one who came to get you out of the meeting the day the police came.'

'Oh, heavens, him!' Isabel murmured.

'He didn't say if there was a problem. It did sound rather urgent though,' Esther admitted.

Isabel sighed. There was enough to worry about without unexpected work difficulties cropping up. 'OK,' she told Esther, aiming for cheery briskness. 'I'll pop along to see him now. Would you open the post and check through it for me?'

'Fine,' said Esther.

'No, on second thoughts,' Isabel said turning at the door, 'leave the snail mail for me to open. Boot up my computer first and check the emails, would you?'

Esther looked at her curiously. 'Yes, of course. That's no problem.'

Isabel stood in the lift, thinking about her reluctance to let Esther open the post and wondering if she herself would ever open another letter with casual interest. She supposed that after her experience with the razor blade, there would always be the lingering fear that she, or her staff, could be harmed by the simple task of tearing open an envelope.

She was ushered into the senior partner's office by his glamorous, and somewhat fierce, personal assistant.

'Good morning, Mr Brown.' Isabel said, with as cheerful smile as she could manage as her boss rose to his feet.

'Ah! Isabel. Thank you very much for coming along so promptly. Do please sit down.'

He went to sit in the huge leather chair behind his desk, folded his hands into a steeple and looked grave.

What now? wondered Isabel. Have I made some dreadful error of judgement? Have I lost a prestigious client millions? Or has Gareth Brown found something out about the reason for Max's visit? The now familiar-anxiety which had become her constant companion leapt through her nerves.

'I know this will come as rather a surprise, Isabel,' Gareth Brown said carefully. 'I have a crucial meeting in Paris this afternoon and I'd very much like to take a colleague along with me for advice and support. I didn't know about the meeting until late yesterday evening, which is why I'm asking you at such short notice.' He looked at her with a quizzical smile.

Isabel jerked into alertness. Surely this was unusual, irregular even. Senior partners usually operated solo at key meetings, or took along their Personal Assistants.

'You're looking somewhat sceptical,' the man ventured with a faint smile.

'Yes,' Isabel admitted. 'I was wondering what precisely would be the kind of advice and support you're looking for. And if I'm the right person to give it?' And whether you're trying to come on to me, she added to herself silently, rather startled to think of the very correct, somewhat staid Gareth Brown in the role of seducer.

'We're looking at the possibilities of taking over a Parisian brokers,' Brown explained. 'It's all at a very preliminary stage. Naturally, I'd value the opinion of someone as gifted as yourself regarding investment and risk.'

'I see,' Isabel said slowly. She was still suspicious. Her skills lay in advising clients about personal investments – business takeovers and mergers were not her scene at all.

'Is there some problem, Isabel?' Her boss wondered, looking somewhat beady. 'Of course, I appreciate that you have been having some difficulties recently, as you were kind enough to inform me. But you did assure me these issues would not interfere in any way with your work.'

'No, No of course not,' Isabel assured him. She tried to think things through, wondering what the implications of leaving the country were as regards the plans she had agreed to with Max and his team. As was often the case at the moment, her mind seemed full of cloud and mist.

'We do like to feel that our employees are one hundred percent committed to the job and ready to be flexible,' Gareth Brown reminded her. 'I realise this trip would mean your working through into the evening. And, no doubt, there will be entertainment laid on afterwards which we should be obliged to attend as a matter of courtesy. But we shall be flying back to London tomorrow morning. Your routine would not be severely disrupted.'

Isabel had a sense that she was being put to some kind of test and that it would be very unwise, in terms of her career prospects to refuse this proposed trip to Paris. Moreover, if Brown had other motives than work in mind and started to get amorous, she was pretty confident of being able to cope with him. It wouldn't be the first time a senior colleague had tried some elaborate dodge to get her into bed with him.

'Of course I'd be delighted to come along on behalf of the firm, Mr Brown,' she told him brightly.

'Gareth,' he smiled back at her. He gave a little cough. 'I've always wished my parents had called me James,' he added with a twinkly smile. 'But there we are, we have to live with what is handed out to us.'

Phew! thought Isabel, escaping from Brown's office and heading back to her own. Off to Paris with Gareth Brown who wishes he were James! Didn't she have enough troubles already?

Esther thought it was great news. 'Are you sure he doesn't want me to come along as well? I could look after you both, make sure you have all the relevant documents to hand. And act as chaperone!' she added mischievously.

'This is strictly business,' Isabel said severely.

'Ho, ho,' Esther murmured meaningfully as she waltzed back to her own office.

Isabel left work at lunchtime and went back to her flat. She threw her soft, leather case on the bed and began to pack. Underwear, nightwear, shoes and make-up went in first. She would need to take an extra work suit, and also something to wear in the evening, if there were to be some kind of social gathering. She chose a long, silky black crepe dress and a beaded emerald jacket.

Once her case was zipped up and standing in the hallway, she paused before ringing for a taxi to take her to Heathrow. She needed to let Max know where she was going, that she would be out of the country for twenty-four hours. After some consideration, she supposed she could simply ask the officer in the watch car outside to pass on the message to him. No, that was too cold, too clinical. She wanted to tell him herself. Explain the situation.

She wanted to hear his voice, for goodness sake.

She called his mobile number but his phone was switched off, so there was no alternative but to leave a message on voicemail. She knew she had to be careful, but it was so hard to leave a cool, bare-bones message of her whereabouts without giving any personal details or explanations. Without being able to add a loving farewell. But mobile phones were notoriously unsafe. It was so easy for someone else to pick one up if it had been left lying around. Tap into messages…

The taxi hooted as it arrived. As Isabel opened the door and pushed her case through, the officer in the waiting police car leapt out and hurried down the steps.

'I'll take that, madam,' he said courteously. 'Might I ask where you're going? How long you'll be away?'

'Thank you,' Isabel said, handing over the case. She was grateful for his help and concern, yet at the same time faintly resentful of having her every movement tracked as though she – herself – were some kind of criminal. Crisply she gave the officer the information he had requested, then thanked him again as he loaded her case into the taxi and closed the door behind her.

'Heathrow,' she told the driver, noticing the surprise on his face at the little pantomime that had just taken place.

They drove along in silence for a while. It was a grey afternoon with cold little spits of rain in the air. The taxi driver switched on the wipers and washed the screen. He then peered into his rear-view mirror.

'We seem to have a police escort, miss,' he observed in sardonic tones.

'Yes. I just don't seem able to shake them off at the moment,' Isabel told him, matching the driver's own irony. 'But I can assure you I'm neither armed nor dangerous!'

He made no comment, concentrating on weaving the car through the jumble of London traffic, now building up towards the tea-time rush hour.

Gareth Brown was waiting for her in the Departure Hall. Isabel greeted him, then looked behind her to see if the police car was still outside. It was something of a relief to find that the police vehicle had become snarled in a jam at the exit to one of the airport's massive car parks. Even the switching on of the siren and blue lights did little to help its progress. At long last, she was free to go wherever she wanted without being tracked.

A tiny spark of excitement flared inside her at the thought of this unexpected visit to Paris. Of flying off into the bright – cobalt sky – above the clouds. Leaving all the horror of the monster's harassment behind her for a few hours.

'I've checked us in,' Gareth told her. 'Let's go straight through to the VIP lounge and have a glass of champagne.'

Isabel glanced swiftly back towards the entry doors. The police car had drawn up at the entrance now and was parked on the double yellow lines. The officer was getting out, but she and Gareth were already passing through passport and security control. Surely the officer wouldn't track her any further.

As they sipped champagne in the VIP lounge, she kept glancing at the door, but no tracker appeared.

'How come we're VIPs?' she asked Gareth Brown..

'My wife is a junior cabinet minister.' He smiled. 'Good contacts are so helpful, don't you think?'

'Yes,' she murmured, thinking that Gareth's wife must be a powerful and very busy woman. And wondering if poor Gareth was feeling neglected and sex-starved!

On the flight Gareth behaved impeccably, filling her in on the reasons behind the possible take-over of the Parisian broking firm, pulling explanatory documents from his case and going through them with her so that she would be fully briefed for the meeting. The polite and perfect boss.

They took the City Express from Charles de Gaulle airport and then a taxi to the brokers' offices in the heart of Paris' commercial sector.

Landmarks flashed by – the solidity of the Arc de Triomph, a glimpse of the delicate ironwork of the Eiffel Tower stretching up to a pale-blue sky. Lowering the window a little, she heard the hum and hooting of the traffic, caught the pungent smell of hot diesel fumes mingled with the unique and unmistakable fragrance of French cigarettes.

'Mmm, there's no other city quite like Paris,' Gareth murmured, smiling at Isabel and raising his eyebrows.

The meeting was held in a conference room very much like the one at Isabel's firm in London. There were four directors and two departmental managers present, one of whom was a gorgeous, leggy blonde who reminded Isabel of Brigitte Bardot in her younger days. The meeting was conducted in French as Gareth spoke the language faultlessly. Isabel found she had to concentrate hard for, although she was a competent French speaker, she was not quite as skilled or practised as her boss.

After an hour, coffee and cakes were provided and the atmosphere became slightly more relaxed. Isabel was just beginning to feel she was getting a full grasp on the proceedings, when the door opened and a tall dark man walked in quietly and sat down on one of the chairs arranged around the walls.

Isabel stared at him in disbelief. Max! She simply could not believe it. She kept on staring at him as though he were an illusion, a shadow that might just melt away as she watched it. It took a few moments for the reality to register and then sink in. Max, here in Paris. Her heart felt as though it would spring out of her chest, it was beating so frantically.

His eyes connected with hers, stern and direct.

She realised she should never have dreamed of coming here to Paris without checking with him personally first. She was under his protection – he was responsible for her safety and, if anything should happen to her, he would carry the can. She cursed herself for not thinking things through more carefully.

Her legs shook as she stood up. She walked around the table and, bending down to Gareth, she murmured brief apologies and then walked to the door, her eyes avoiding Max in an attempt to make it seem to the people around the conference table that his sudden appearance had nothing to do with her leaving the meeting.

She stood outside the door, shivering slightly although the building was tropically warm.

An eternity seemed to pass and then Max stepped through the door to join her. He said nothing, simply stood very close to her, his eyes holding hers. And just for a moment the power of his presence almost frightened her.

'I'm sorry,' she whispered, 'I should have made sure to speak to you about this before I set off.'

'Yes,' he agreed. 'You should.'

Oh hell! This calm, stern disapproval was far worse

than being shouted out. She tried desperately to find a way to put things right with Max. 'I just thought I would be quite safe once I was away from London. And one of our firm's senior partners was with me all the time. I wasn't in any danger.'

'I don't suppose it occurred to you that this senior partner you refer to could be the man who is harassing you!' Max looked down at her, his eyes like guns.

'No, of course not!' she protested. 'Don't be ridiculous, he's been with the firm for years. He's rock-solid respectable and completely trustworthy.' She gazed at Max, her eyes wide and pleading. 'His wife's a government minister.'

'And you think that rules him out of our list of possible suspects?' Max enquired coldly.

'Well, no.' Wings of colour mounted in her cheeks as she realised how stupid she had been. 'I suppose not,' she concluded lamely.

'I've known murderers who were so outwardly squeaky-clean, your grandmother would have eaten her dinner off them,' he said grimly. 'But the mutilated corpses they left in their wake were a different matter.'

'Yes.' She nodded miserably.

'And what were you thinking of deliberately – avoiding the officer who had been detailed to keep a watch on you? To keep you safe. He called me whilst you were on your way to the airport to tell me what was happening. I told him not to let you get on that plane, under any circumstances, unless there was a police officer accompanying you.' He gave an exasperated sigh. 'And all you could think of was to play hide-and-seek. Oh, Isabel!'

'I just wanted to feel – free,' she said, tears pricking her eyelids.

There was a beating pause. 'Yes. Don't think I haven't guessed.' Suddenly his tone and his mood had changed. 'This is all awful for you, Isabel, feeling that you're under constant surveillance. But you've got to try to keep a cool, clear head, and not fight against my efforts to keep you alive and safe, however restricting they might seem.'

'I know. Oh, Max, I'm so sorry. I never meant to give you all this hassle.'

'Yes, I do understand,' he said, his voice low and caressing. He paused for a few moments. 'So, here I am, at the end of a wild goose chase and at a loose end in a foreign capital. What can you do to make it up to me, Isabel?' His eyes were suddenly lit with a sparkle of teasing challenge.

'Well…' Her voice caught in her throat.

'What time does your meeting end?' he asked crisply.

'I'm not sure.'

'It makes no difference. I'm willing to wait,' he said. He shot her a meaningful glance, making her pulses jump. 'After all, here we are in the most romantic city in the world, just the two of us. Why waste a marvellous opportunity?'

Just as Isabel was thinking of a reply, Gareth emerged from the meeting room, his expression betraying that he was both suspicious and not best-pleased.

'You again!' he exclaimed to Max.

'I must apologise for any disruption,' Max said quietly. 'But I have to tell you that my presence here is both necessary and justified.'

'I see, Inspector,' Gareth said slowly. He frowned, perplexed. 'And are you planning to – how shall I put it – detain Isabel? To take her back to London with you?'

Why didn't he just add 'in handcuffs' Isabel thought

with an internal sigh.

'Miss Bruce is not under any suspicion,' Max informed Gareth, his face closed and severe. He glanced at Isabel, giving her the opportunity to speak if she wished but she simply stared straight ahead, biting her lip in uncertainty.

Gareth looked between the two of them in growing bewilderment.

'Miss Bruce has been receiving disturbing threats from an anonymous letter writer,' Max told Gareth. 'We believe the person making these threats is both determined and dangerous, and that he could well have followed her here to Paris. All in all, we have sufficient evidence to lead us to believe she would be safer under police protection back in the UK.'

'Good heavens!' Gareth exclaimed, after a short pause. 'Why didn't you tell me this Isabel? How dreadful for you. But surely it would have been better all round if you had trusted me with this information?'

'Yes,' she agreed miserably. It was so hard to explain to people how tainted and shamed you felt at being placed in the role of victim, how you longed to keep it buried and secret. 'I'm truly sorry, Gareth. Please believe me.'

The door of the conference room opened once again and the Brigitte Bardot-style blonde slid through, her glance running over the solemn trio standing in the corridor.

'Is everything all right?' she asked Gareth in a deliciously-low, husky voice, her huge brown eyes full of concern.

'In the main, yes,' he assured her. 'However, we do seem to have a slight problem. It looks as though Miss Bruce will have to leave us and return to London without delay.'

'Oh dear!' She turned to Isabel. 'Oh, how very unfortunate. You will miss the lovely party we had planned for you and Gareth tonight. That is such a shame.'

'Yes, I'm sorry,' Isabel said, feeling as if she were a mechanical doll programmed to do nothing but apologise.

'Well, it cannot be helped,' the Bardot doppelganger said sympathetically. She smiled up at Gareth her eyes full of invitation. 'Will you soon be re-joining us in the meeting, Gareth?'

He nodded and, giving a worried farewell smile to Isabel and a brief nod to Max, followed her back into the conference room.

'I think he'll be quite happy without you,' Max observed in dry tones, looking quizzically at Isabel. 'And for the record, I don't regard him as a suspect.'

'No, I'm sure he's not. And I don't think he's a wolf on the prowl either. I rather get the impression he was simply hoping for a bit of a break and a little fun away from the pressures of his job in London and lonely evenings sitting at home waiting for his wife to come home from the House of Commons.' Isabel was pretty sure Gareth was basically a nice guy who had just wanted to enjoy some light-hearted relaxation. She shouldn't have doubted his motives. But then, at present, she seemed suspicious of nearly everyone on some count or other.

'Well as long as he wasn't hoping to have a little fun with *you,'* Max commented grimly. 'I would have personally strangled him and thrown his body in the Seine if I'd arrived to find him trying to engineer a flirtatious one-night stand.'

Isabel flushed. 'Don't even think it, Max! You know I would never have allowed things to get out of hand. And anyway, I think Gareth will be kept extremely busy and happy with the Miss Bardot lookalike, don't you?'

He smiled. 'Yes, I hope he will,' he said softly. 'And what about you and me? I'm signed out of the station until noon tomorrow.' His eyes connected with hers, full of suggestion and promise. 'So – are you free this evening, Miss Bruce?' he enquired with velvet irony.

A dark thrill chased through Isabel at the thought of a whole evening and night alone with Max in a strange city where there would be no prying eyes watching them. 'I think I could be persuaded to cancel all my other engagements, Inspector,' she told him demurely.

He smiled. 'Oh, my sweet love,' he murmured.

'On one condition,' she added softly.

His eyes sharpened. 'What?'

'That we don't say one single word about my "case". That we forget all about the monster and our plans to catch him. That just for one night, we are simply two people in love, spending time together for the very simple reason that we adore each other.' Her eyes were lit with challenge. 'Do you promise?'

He nodded. 'I promise.' He put his arm around her and propelled her down to the street where he hailed a taxi. 'The Paris Cameo near La Madeleine,' he told the driver.

The traffic was appalling. Cars were bumper-to-bumper in every street. Drivers yelled swear-words at each other through their open windows as they swerved to overtake in spaces barely wide enough for a bicycle. 'Paris is becoming a nightmare,' Max murmured softly so as not offend the driver. 'Even worse than London. Dog-eat-dog is the only way to drive. Storm your way through regardless.'

'Reckless daring,' Isabel smiled. 'Like the French cavalry in the Napoleonic wars.'

'Don't stop to assess the damage,' Max grinned. 'And never, never stop at a zebra-crossing unless there's a policeman on it. Heaven help the poor chap!'

Isabel laughed. 'Ssh, we'll be had up for treason and sent to the guillotine.'

When they reached the bistro it was already crowded. The atmosphere was humming with voices and filled with the scent of garlic and wonderful fish sauces.

They ordered scallops cooked in white wine, followed by tender lamb cutlets served with a simple green salad. Whilst they were waiting for their food, they drank Sancerre and Isabel nibbled on a freshly-baked baguette.

'This is heaven!' she exclaimed, staring across the table into Max's beautifully stern face.

'We must just hope Gareth and company don't turn up here for their party and rumble us,' he said dryly.

'No need to worry,' she smiled. 'The party's at the house of one of the directors in a hugely chic apartment near the Tour Montparnasse. I think we're safe. At long last.' She put her hand over his. The prospect of making love with him again had made her body come alive. She imagined them once more crushed against each other, their hearts thudding, the blood pulsing wildly between them.

When the food arrived, it looked and tasted delicious, but anticipation at being with Max had killed her appetite, even though she had eaten very little all day. Her stomach was empty and yet it was almost impossible for her to eat the food. She simply longed to be alone with him, to give herself to him without any restraint.

Eventually the waiter brought the bill and accepted Max's handful of Francs with grave thanks. 'We hope to see you again very soon, Monseuir,' he said, in carefully-enunciated English. 'It is too long since we last had the pleasure of serving you.'

Isabel had the impression Max had once been a regular customer at the restaurant and she was very conscious of the waiter's interested glance in her direction.

'Did you used to come here with your wife?' she asked Max tentatively, as they walked out into the cool evening air.

He nodded. 'Yes.' She waited for him to say more, but he was silent and she wished she had not asked. She wondered when would be the right time for him to talk to her about Jennifer. She knew it was not now, but she hoped it would be soon.

'That was a lovely, lovely dinner,' she told him, taking his arm. 'Thank you.'

'Thank you for being there with me. For laying ghosts,' he said reflectively. Then, before she could follow up his remark, he asked, 'Your place or mine?' and his tone was dry and ironic and just a touch seductive. Suddenly she forgot all about Jennifer, all about the past. All that mattered was the here and now. With Max.

'Yours,' she smiled. 'We don't want our style cramped by having Gareth just down the corridor in my hotel, do we?'

Isabel could hardly wait until they were alone together. But when they entered the unfamiliar, impersonal hotel bedroom she felt a sudden shyness. She watched Max cross to the dressing table and place his keys carefully on its glass top. He turned to her, standing quite still, his face solemn and full of feeling.

She had a strong sense of the strength of his male need for her. And of her own desire to please him. To tease and seduce him like a beautiful Parisian courtesan tempting her lover. Standing a little distance from him, she slowly unfastened the zip of her dress.

He watched her, his eyes dark with emotion. He took a step towards her but she moved back from him, holding his gaze with her own level stare. Lingeringly, she lowered her dress to the floor then stepped out of it. Beneath she wore nothing but matching oyster satin bra, skimpy briefs and lacy hold-up stockings.

Max let out a long, groaning sigh.

With long slow movements she gracefully took off the rest of her clothes. When she was naked, she stood very still, her hands resting against her sides, letting him take his fill of her smooth, creamy-skinned body. Only the sound of her breathing, the rise and fall of her breasts revealed her true emotions.

'You are so beautiful,' Max murmured, looking at her breasts which were the colour of ivory, their aureoles dark and wide, her nipples rosy pink and already erect. His eyes moved over the long, perfect sweep from her thighs to her curved hips and her narrow waist. She had the beautiful voluptuousness of a woman in her prime, whose femininity was both delicate and fully ripe.

She moved to stand beside him and placed herself close against him, taking his hands and laying them on her breasts, offering her mouth for him to kiss. For a while, she allowed him simply to look at her, unselfconscious and without any shame or awkwardness. Then her body curved towards him as she was drawn to his warmth and the strength of his desire. In a gesture of gentle female surrender, she tipped her head languorously backwards and presented him with her throat, exposed and vulnerable.

As he kissed her she began to undress him, bending to

kiss him in return, swooping over his chest and stomach and thighs as his body was gradually freed from its clothes.

'I've felt hollow for so long,' he murmured. 'I tried to tell myself sex didn't matter. That love was no longer possible.'

'Love is everything,' Isabel told him. 'I shall never forget that. Not since making love with you, Max, my own darling.'

He carried her to the bed and laid her down on the covers. She raised her arms above her head and parted her legs slightly. 'I feel like a nude in a lush Italian painting,' she smiled. 'All warm and golden and dishevelled.'

His face was between her breasts, his lips moving to suck first one nipple and then the other. She pulled his head up so their lips could meet again. Her breathing was accelerating and she felt herself opening up, body and soul, ready to give herself to him totally and absolutely.

His eyes were moving over her hair, taking in its deep-auburn lustre and weight. She moved her hand and lazily pulled out the handful of long pins that held her hair in a neat French pleat.

Max reached out and touched the luxurious ripple of the hair as it fell around her shoulders and on to the pillow. His hands moved from the crown of her head down the shining length of the glossy strands. A sigh shuddered through his body.

Suddenly she raised herself up and kissed his lips with a primitive ferocity that had him gasping. His response was instant, and soon they were kissing with tense urgency, their mood darkening in tune with the hot flood of their desire.

Isabel loved the tangy, masculine flavour that was

uniquely Max. He tasted of deep green woods torn with winds and rain blowing from a salty sea. She suddenly felt utterly wild and abandoned. Her hand moved to cradle his maleness and she cried aloud with an overwhelming desire to please him. To give him a taste of ecstasy.

And at the same time, his hands were moving over her, butterfly-tender into each curve and crevice, making her sigh with pleasure to be touched by a man with such exquisite sensitivity.

As his lips began to follow the path his fingers had taken, she felt herself suddenly melting, powerless to do anything but lie back and let him arouse a storm of emotion and sensation which she knew would rock her to her very bones.

She heard low growls of desire weaving through the air around them, soft moans of pleasure, but which were his and which were hers it was hard to tell.

Moaning softly, she arched herself against him, clutching at him, grasping him hungrily and taking him inside her. And then there was no other sensation except Max and his hard, insistent thrusts, binding her to him, making her his own for ever.

Time stopped. There was just a long golden tunnel of pleasure through which she was spinning, on and on, the joy reverberating, humming, echoing.

She heard herself let out a long, low animal cry. The incandescent shower of sensation that followed left her dazed, gasping and spent.

Max rolled himself to lie beside her, pushed back the damp strands of hair clinging to her face and kissed both her temples with lingering tenderness. They held hands and let the drowsy peace of spent passion wash over them.

After an hour or so, Max rang room service and ordered champagne.

They drank it sitting up naked in bed. He dipped a finger in the bubbles and traced a pattern over Isabel's breast. Then he dipped his finger in once again and this time traced it around her navel, moving steadily downwards.

And then they made love again, this time slow and voluptuous, their eyes holding each other.

She slept in the enclosure of his arms and when she woke, he was waiting for her, leaning on one elbow and looking down at her, his eyes brimming with love and desire.

When they eventually left for the airport, she found herself aching, bruised and utterly satisfied. She reached for his hand as they waited in the queue at the check-in. His fingers curled themselves reassuringly around hers, making her smile with pleasure. But when she looked into his face she saw that there was a new tightness there which had not been in evidence the evening before. During their stay in Paris, he had, for a few brief moments, been able to forget the burdens and responsibilities of his work. But now she could see that the tension and strain which comes from doing a job demanding total commitment was slowly filtering back into his system.

'What happens next?' she asked as they winged their way back to Heathrow.

'We go on with our plan to flush out the man who's making your life a misery,' he said grimly. 'And with no more delays.'

'I'd almost forgotten about him,' she said sadly. 'We had such a wonderful, beautiful time together didn't we? In Paris we seemed to be in another life, another world.'

'Yes,' he agreed. 'But sadly it was just a small interlude.'

As they started their descent into London, she could see the line of his jaw stiffening. It was almost as though he were gradually withdrawing from her, opening up a distance between them. Max, the upholder of the law. Isabel, the victim of a cruel pursuer.

The spontaneous warmth and tenderness he had shown her in France all seemed to be melting away. She looked down sadly at the grey landscape of England as they came through the clouds.

Paris seemed like no more than a dream. An idyll, offering a brief escape from the grim reality of what they had to face on their return to London.

chapter twelve

What does a girl wear for a blind date? Isabel asked herself as she looked along the row of clothes in her wardrobe. She took out a green silk suit, then put it back and considered the merits of a lilac shirt with flared navy trousers. In the end, she decided on a simple black dress with a long slender skirt and narrow shoulder straps.

She knew what others saw when they looked at her: white, translucent skin, large eyes so skilfully made-up, no one would know there was any artificial colour, hair shiny and classically twisted into a neat, secure pleat, discreet pearl earrings and finally glossy black high-heels, meant for elegant interiors, not the streets.

She frowned. The whole image was altogether too uptight. 'No, no,' she murmured, pulling off the dainty stud earrings and abandoning them on the dressing table. She slid the securing pins from her hair and let it fall loose around her shoulders. Ahh! That was better.

She looked in her jewellery case and examined its contents.

What am I doing agonising over the image I'm trying to create, she thought, recalling Max's directive that she simply be herself.

Smiling ruefully she lifted out some pearl-and-diamond drop earrings that had belonged to her grandmother. They were Victorian, large and important-looking and she guessed they were quite valuable. She put them on, then went to the mirror turning her head and admiring the soft gleam of the pear-shaped pearls, the twinkle of the diamonds encrusting the studs that supported them. The earrings were quality items with just a touch of ostentation.

'You'll do fine,' she told her reflection.

Her stomach felt fluttery and hollow and she hoped she would be able to eat something when the dinner arrived. If not, she supposed she could always plead nerves. And then she thought of Max and her courage soared. He would be there for her at the restaurant, ensuring her safety and her well-being. She could not sit by him, nor even acknowledge him, but he would be *there.* She would feel his closeness, the bliss of simply being in his presence. Through all her apprehension, a flame of anticipation flickered within.

She checked her watch. There were fifteen minutes to go before the taxi came for her. A taxi loaned from a private firm on Max's instructions and driven by an officer posing as a cabby.

Everything had been planned down to the last detail. Max had telephoned several times that day, patiently explaining the latest decisions the team had made on procedures. It was like planning a military campaign!

He had advised her to try to keep the reins firmly in her own hands when making arrangements for the meeting, emphasising that it was up to her to suggest times and places, not the man who had responded to her advert. 'But won't he find that rather assertive and unappealing?' she had asked.

'Not if he's familiar with the etiquette of dating through the lonely hearts columns,' he explained. 'It's normal practice for the person who has placed the advert to make the decisions.'

He was right. When she had contacted the man she was to meet that evening, he had made the assumption she would call the shots on when and where they should meet. He had also sounded very sure of himself and Isabel had been doubtful that he fitted with the picture Max had painted of a lonely, socially-inept man.

Max's team had decided on a newly-opened. French-style restaurant about ten minutes' drive from Isabel's flat as a meeting place. There would be heavy security on her behalf throughout the meeting with her dinner ‚date'. Jack Cheney was to be posing as one of the restaurant staff. And Max and Emma would be sitting at a nearby table, acting the parts of a loving couple dining out together.

Half-way through the meal Isabel, was to visit the ladies cloakroom, where Emma Hayes would meet her to gather any information and relay this back to Max. Their communications would be done by a code. Brief 'yes' or 'no' answers in response to Emma's innocent-seeming questions. Or, if necessary, a secretly-written note handed over with discretion.

Max's instructions on what should happen on leaving the restaurant had been very clear and very strict. On no account was she to accompany the 'date' anywhere. Not even a few steps down the road. Her 'taxi' would be waiting for her, the same one which had brought her to the restaurant. That was the only vehicle she must get into, on no account must she be persuaded to get in to any other! She was not to make any commitments to meet the man again, but to leave things open and casually friendly so as not to arouse suspicions. And if there were any problems at all, Max would step in.

Isabel checked her watch again – only one minute had gone by! She took deep breaths, cursing herself for being ready too early and leaving time for anxiety to take a crippling hold on her.

The door buzzer sounded and her insides suddenly felt molten with fear. Swallowing hard she went down the hallway. 'Who is it?'

'Police, madam. From Inspector Hawthorne's team.'

She pulled on the chain and opened the door a fraction. A cheery-looking, uniformed male officer stood there, and behind him she was vaguely aware of two hovering figures hidden in the shadows.

'You have visitors, madam,' the officer told her. 'A lady who says she's your sister. She's with her boy-friend.'

'Darling!' came Luisa's voice. 'It's me and Josh!'

Isabel sagged against the door frame in relief. 'It's all right,' she told the officer, 'They're genuine. But thanks for checking, anyway.'

'Just doing my job, madam,' he smiled, turning and tramping back up the steps.

'Izzie, sweetheart, what the hell's going on?' exclaimed Luisa as Isabel ushered her and Josh inside. She looked at Isabel curiously. 'Oh, are you going out? You're all dressed up?'

'Yes, in a few minutes. Hi, Josh!' Isabel smiled up at Josh, noticing how white and sparkly his teeth were when he smiled.

'Hi! You're looking great Isabel,' he said grinning at her appreciatively. 'Who's the lucky guy?'

'Aha,' Isabel said lightly, leading the way through to the sitting-room and pouring a gin and tonic which was Luisa's standard drink. Josh's eyes twinkled when he said he would have one too.

'But Izzie,' Luisa insisted, her eyes clouded with worry,

'why are the police outside? What's all that about? Oh, are you OK, sweetheart?'

Isabel pinned on a smile and made it stick. 'I'm simply fine, Luisa. There's no need to worry.' She forced her brain to work – and fast. 'There have some problems for me and the person in the flat above recently. Nuisance calls, threats and so on. The police are quite keen to catch whoever it is.'

Luisa looked doubtful. 'Well, it all seemed rather heavy to me. They wouldn't even let us come and knock on the door until they'd checked with you.'

'I suppose that makes sense,' Isabel said calmly. 'They can't rule anyone out, can they?'

'I suppose not.' Luisa glanced worriedly at Josh. He smiled back at her and mouthed a kiss. 'So, who did you say you were going out with?' she asked Isabel. 'Is this a hot date?'

'Just a casual dinner date. He's a sort of friend of a friend. He's in management consulting. He seems nice enough.'

'Oh!' Luisa exclaimed with a small grimace. 'In other words, you're keeping him a secret.'

'Just for the moment,' Isabel agreed. 'I don't really know very much about him yet. Where are you two off to?' she asked, turning the spotlight back on to her sister.

'A smart party in the West End. I'm hoping to impress a TV producer, and, of course, show Josh off and make everyone jealous as hell. We just called in to say hello, Izzie.' Luisa looked at her sister with such affection that Isabel went up to her and gave her a hug.

'You're looking lovely,' Isabel told her, thinking that Luisa was fantastically resilient. No one would guess she had recently undergone the trauma of an abortion.

'Have you spoken to Father recently?' she asked Luisa.

Instantly Luisa's face hardened. 'I rang yesterday. He could only speak to me for a minute or so, said he had an "appointment".'

'Did you know he was going into hospital in a day or so?'

'No,' responded Luisa. 'I've told you, he never tells me anything these days.'

'He's having some tests. Some problem with his heart.'

'Very apt,' Luisa said with irony. 'He's always had problems in that direction. Sorry, I didn't mean to sound bitchy. Is it serious?'

'I don't know,' Isabel said. 'He's being very stiff-upper-lip about it.'

'Well, we shall just have to wait and see, shan't we darling?' Luisa put her glass down and glanced towards Josh. 'Time to go sweetie?'

Josh looked back ruefully at Isabel as Luisa swept through the door, clearly not wanting to hear any more on the subject of their father.

'Oh, Luisa!' Isabel murmured regretfully. 'And oh, Father too!' They were both equally unbending and stubborn towards each other. Isabel reminded herself that there was little she could do to patch things up between them. The wounds had gone beyond mere sticking-plaster.

She looked up into the road above, seeing the lights of a taxi flare as it parked beside the curb. Her driver was a young woman, who showed her badge, introduced herself as a member of Inspector Hawthorne's team and then drove Isabel with swift efficiency to the designated restaurant.

'Here goes!' Isabel murmured as she climbed from the car.

'Good-bye, and good luck,' whispered the driver.

Isabel walked slowly up the wrought-iron staircase leading to the first-floor restaurant. Golden light spilled from the windows and, as she approached the glass entrance doors, a figure sprang forward to open them for her.

'Good evening, Madam,' said PC Cheney, smiling impartially as though they had never met before. Isabel handed him her swirling green cape. She looked towards the small corner bar where the man she was to meet had said he would be waiting. He had told her his name was Jeremy, that he had blond hair and that he would be carrying a copy of *The Times*.

There were only a few diners at the bar and Isabel spotted her date immediately. There was no doubt, he was the only blond. Noting that he was busy with the crossword, she took a swift glance around the room to locate Max. Tiny needles of sensation pricked along her spine as she connected with his cool, level gaze. Whilst she had known he would be there watching out for her, the brief impartial scrutiny of his grey eyes made her intensely conscious of being a woman.

He was sat at a small table with Emma Hayes opposite him, unrecognisably glamorous in a low-cut scarlet dress. She saw Max turn his attention back to Emma, leaning towards her across the table as though they were lovers. Lucky Emma.

She felt a hand on her elbow, and heard a soft, seductive voice. 'You must be Isabel, yes? I'm Jeremy.'

She looked up, pulling herself out of her thoughts, startled a little and blushing. 'Oh! Jeremy.' Oh, God! she thought panic-stricken, what do I say next?

'Come and have a drink,' he said invitingly. 'I've

ordered champagne. Nothing to beat the real thing, eh? Oh, and by the way, let's get things straight right from the start. This evening is on me. So forget any of that "going Dutch" nonsense.'

There was no need for her to have worried about making small talk. Jeremy seemed like a practised professional. Whilst she sipped her ice-cold champagne, he gave her a brief potted history of his life. He had been to public school, then Oxbridge. He was a carefree bachelor but looking around for the right woman! This last snippet of information was accompanied by a seductive lift of his very sleek eyebrows which looked as though they had been professionally shaped at a beauty salon.

Isabel responded with a little about her own family and briefly told him about her job.

'I like high-fliers,' he said with satisfaction. 'Women with brains and initiative.' He leaned towards her with some more eyebrow juggling. 'Some men feel threatened by female success,' he smiled. 'Can't think why. A little competition can add a very interesting spark to a relationship.'

They moved to their table, escorted with admirable professionalism by PC Cheney. It was three tables away from the one Max and Emma were sharing. Close, but not quite close enough for conversations to be overheard. Thank Heavens for that, thought Isabel, alarmed by the thought of Max making an assessment of each word she uttered.

Jeremy made a swift perusal of the wine list, ordered further champagne, then opened the menu.

Whilst they were occupied in choosing their food, Isabel found herself glancing at him from-time-to time wondering if he was a man who entertained himself by sending a woman menacing 'gifts'. A man who could fantasise about taking an unknown woman to the limits of pain, and write and tell her so! A man who attacked women in the street and made their faces look like punch-bags. No, she decided. He hasn't the guts for it. He's a lounge lizard, a man used to luxury and pampering. And then almost instantly she changed her mind. Anyone had that potential. There was no 'type', no obvious human traits one could spot a mile off.

'You're looking thoughtful,' said Jeremy. 'What's on your mind?'

'Oh...' she shrugged suggestively. 'This and that.'

'Secrets,' he grinned. 'I love secrets, especially those of beautiful women. Most particularly those with such gorgeous, sexy red hair!'

Isabel breathed in and gave him a deeply mysterious smile.

'Tell me,' he said, 'why does a lovely lady like you need to advertise to get a man to take her to dinner?'

'Well,' she responded in confessional tones, 'when you're a woman on your own in London with a high-profile career, it can sometimes be rather...lonely.' She realised she was telling the honest truth, at least as far as her life before she met Max was concerned.

Jeremy laid a hand over hers. 'Poor lonely Isabel. But now you've found me, things will all be different. I think we could get along rather well. Mmm?' The eyebrows were now performing quite stunning gymnastics!

Their food arrived, a starter of roasted peppers and goats cheese drizzled with oil and lemon. Watching Jeremy attack his food, Isabel felt fairly sure that he would expect her to join in a bout of athletic sex to round off to the evening, and that he would not be easy to put off. She glanced in Max's direction for reassurance. But he and Emma were engrossed in conversation. It was hard to believe they were keeping a close watch on her.

'I'm working for a management company at the moment,' Jeremy told her, 'but I've got plans for setting up on my own very soon.'

'Exciting but risky,' Isabel commented with a smile. 'And requiring a good deal of capital, I would imagine.'

'Yes, indeed! Frightening amounts. Don't worry, Isabel, there's no shortage of rich folks willing to back me.' The eyebrows wiggled suggestively.

As Isabel listened politely, she was aware of a woman's figure bursting through the door, pausing and then heading straight for their table. She looked up, startled. The woman was small and dark and pretty. She was wearing blue dungarees and looked around seven months pregnant. She also looked incandescent with fury.

'What the hell do you think you're playing at?' she yelled at Jeremy. She flung out her hand and struck him across the cheek. 'You pig! You utter, loathsome, stinking swine!'

Jeremy held up his hands in surrender. 'Now look, darling. This is just a business meeting…'

'You expect me to buy that old chestnut? I may be a brood mare but I haven't lost my wits.' She turned to Isabel. 'And I'm sorry for you, whoever you are. You picked the wrong guy. Or do you make a habit of dining out with married blokes?'

Isabel stared in consternation at Jeremy's enraged wife, feeling herself blush with dismay and squirming embarrassment.

'Well!' the tiny dark woman challenged Jeremy, 'are you coming home with me now because, if not, I can tell you I'll be filing for a divorce. And I think Daddy's promise of finance for the new business will be vanishing into thin air.'

Jeremy leapt up, his smooth features crumpled with alarm. 'OK, I get the message. Calm down sweetie. I'm coming. Right now.' He pulled several notes from his wallet. 'Here,' he said to Isabel with an apologetic glance, 'this should cover the damage. So sorry.'

Isabel watched in amazement as Jeremy placed the notes on the table, then with a rueful smile, he took his wife's arm and steered her from the restaurant.

What now? Isabel wondered, standing up and feeling her legs tremble. There was no need to put on an act. Her humiliation following this brief dramatic scene was quite genuine. Staring straight ahead of her and ignoring the curious eyes of the other diners, she made her way to the bar and paid the bill with as much dignity as she could muster.

Outside the air was cold and crisp. She had forgotten her cape, but there was no way she was going back for it. She shivered as she stood at the kerb trying to spot her 'taxi'.

There were footsteps behind her, coming close. She swung round, her pulses electric. 'Max!' she breathed in relief. He had her cape over his arm and with one swift movement, he wrapped it around her shoulders. 'Come on,' he said softly, guiding her towards the 'taxi' which was drawing to a halt beside them.

He gave some brief instructions to the female officer driving, then got into the back of the car with her.

'I can't tell you how sorry I am about all that,' he said grimly.

'It wasn't your fault,' she pointed out.

'Oh yes, I take full responsibility,' he said bitterly. 'I drew up the final list of four men you were to meet and I made a bad misjudgement with that guy.'

'You can't win 'em all, sir,' the officer who was driving remarked.

'Maybe not. But I rather fancy the Superintendent won't be too happy about Miss Bruce having had to endure that tawdry little scene, and all for nothing.'

Isabel turned to him. She could see Max's anger at his mistake stretched over his hawk-like features, chiselled into the tightness of his jaw. With slow, quiet stealth she slid her hand towards his and gave it a firm squeeze.

He turned to look at her. Her heart moved painfully – he was so beautiful. So strong and intensely determined, so utterly desirable. She felt his eyes assessing her and sensed, rather than saw, the question in them. *How can we contrive some plan to be alone together tonight?*

She could feel his need for her, reaching across the correct distance they were forced to keep between him. And she knew that for now, that must be enough to satisfy both of them. On no account was she going to risk putting his career on the line. If they truly loved each other, then they could surely wait until it was safe to allow their commitment to each other to come out in to the open.

When they reached her flat, Max jumped from the car and helped her climb out. He went down the steps with her, followed her through the door and then pulled her into his arms. The pain and ignominy of the evening dissolved and vanished beneath the powerful erotic pleasure of his kiss, the deep, hard pressure of his lips. A huge tremor shot through her body, making her weak with desire and the overwhelming urge to surrender herself to him once again.

She tore herself from the security of his arms. 'We mustn't! It's too dangerous, Max. Your job, your career.'

'To hell with all that,' he said, his eyes hard. 'After what I put you through this evening, I'm not sure how much I deserve to keep it.'

She put a finger over his lips. 'Ssh, you're just saying that in the heat of the moment. You made a minor error in your judgement of a man of whom you knew virtually nothing, on the basis of a single letter. You simply made a wrong guess, Max. Stop judging yourself so harshly.'

'I put you though some hellishly-mortifying moments.' He ran his hands through his hair, pressing his lips together in regret at the memory.

'I'm resilient,' she said, 'I'll bounce back.'

He shook his head. 'No. I've been asking too much of you. You've been under an incredible strain for some time as it is. It was arrogant and wrong of me to expect you to act as a form of human bait, on top of all that, simply to help us nail this guy.' He gave a long sigh. She saw the dark rings of fatigue and remorse beneath his eyes. 'I'm calling the venture off,' he concluded. 'There'll be no more "blind" meetings, no more risks.'

'I want to go on,' Isabel challenged him. 'For my sake, and for the sake of all the other women out there who are at risk from this man and others like him.'

'No.' His eyes were steely and determined. 'I can't allow you to put yourself in jeopardy. I'm calling the project off.'

'If you put a stop to this venture then I think I would have every right to brand you arrogant.'

He shook his head, adamant. She saw how used he was to commanding others, exerting his will over them and getting what he wanted. To be ruthless when it suited him.

She reached out and placed the flat of her hand against his cheek.

'Max,' she said to him with low, soft reasonableness, 'we've only known each other a short time, but because of what we've shared – the dangers and the risks – we know each other better than most people who have been together for ages. Don't you see that?'

She noted that she had caught his full attention, but he offered no response and his eyes still glinted with scepticism.

'In time, we'll be able to be together,' she went on steadily. 'We'll be able to love each other without any restraints or any anxieties about the opinions of other people. You know how much I want you. I want to feel your touch and lie in your arms. And I know you feel just the same.' She looked at him questioningly.

'So?' he said tersely.

'So don't let's fight and spoil these tiny moments of happiness when we're alone together. They're golden moments, too precious to spoil.'

He dropped his arms down by his sides. 'Yes, you're right.' His eyes filled with tenderness as he reached for her again.

'No,' she said, gentle but firm. 'There's an officer waiting for you in the car outside and she'll wonder what we're doing. She'll get suspicious – it's human nature.'

He let her go and let out a long sigh. 'I'll call you tomorrow about the next "date".' He stared hard at her. 'Isabel, are you sure you want to go on with this?'

She smiled sweetly as she held the door for him. 'Are you referring to the "Catch-the-Batterer" project? Or to – Us? Whichever, Max, the answer is a resounding *yes.*'

Max walked slowly up the steps. In his head, he had an image of Isabel as she had looked when she walked into the restaurant earlier that evening. Her face and figure were imprinted on his memory. He recalled noticing that, in profile, her nose was slightly aquiline, but that rather than impairing her loveliness it gave her face character and originality. Her eyes had seemed even more deep-set and luminous within their arched sockets than he had remembered before, the curve of her cheekbones wonderfully defined and as delicate as a woodcarving on a beautiful altar screen.

As she had moved to meet the man who was to later humiliate and abruptly desert her, her breasts had been outlined within her dress – full and round – and he had seen the curve of her thigh as the slit in her skirt parted.

Sitting in the busy restaurant with his knees almost touching those of Emma Hayes, he had felt like a man alone in a gallery staring at a great work of art. And it had come to him with a seismic shock, how very much in love he was with this woman, Isabel.

He recalled her kiss and his heart thundered in his chest.

He slid into the front seat of the car and told the young officer to drive him back to the station. He knew that he should go home and get some sleep, make an early start. He also knew that he needed to think about Isabel, keep her image in his mind's eye, recall the sensation of holding her in his arms.

And once his thoughts and feelings had calmed, then he needed to think very hard about how he was going to protect her from further disasters such as the one he had allowed to befall her earlier.

chapter thirteen

The next evening, Isabel went once again through the rigmarole of dressing, making-up her face and arranging her hair in preparation for meeting a man she had never seen before, who might just turn out to be a vicious criminal.

Despite the fiasco with the philandering Jeremy, she felt calmer this time. She felt she knew the score better, was more prepared for any eventuality, however upsetting. In fact, it was even possible for brief moments to see the black comedy of the whole situation and smile about it.

Ten minutes before her 'taxi' was due she telephoned her father. It was the next morning he was to go into hospital and, whilst she knew he hated her to worry about him, she simply could not let the evening go by without speaking to him.

'No need to fuss, Isabel,' he said predictably. 'I shall be perfectly all right. My usual private-hire man is coming to collect me and Mrs Pringle has packed everything a man could ever need for a short day stay in hospital. I'm doing fine.'

Isabel smiled. 'Of course you are, and of course I need to fuss. That's what daughters are for.'

'Well, some of them maybe, my dear.'

Oh, Heavens, thought Isabel. He's talking about Luisa. I don't suppose she's contacted him in days. Which was hardly surprising when one considered how cold and brusque he could be with his elder child.

'Luisa sends her love,' Isabel said firmly, as though daring him to argue with her. 'She and I were talking about you only yesterday.'

'Hmm,' her father commented. 'And what are you doing with yourself this evening, Isabel?'

'I'm going out to dinner. A very good French-style restaurant in the High Street.'

'Ah,' he said. 'I hope they don't feed you frogs. And with whom are you dining?'

'A friend.' She thought of Max. Love for him beat in her blood, pounding unstoppable.

'Of the male or female species?'

'Male.'

A pause. 'I see. And shall I be meeting him in due course?'

'I hope so Father, I really do.'

After she had put the phone down, she parted the curtains and saw that her 'taxi' was waiting. There was a curious sense of deja-vu as she climbed in and greeted the driver, as she watched the tail-lights of the cars in front as they drove through the traffic then stopped at the restaurant, as she walked up the iron staircase, swept through the door and gave Jack Cheney her green cape.

But this evening, she had the impression that the constable gave her an especially lingering quizzical glance as he welcomed her to the restaurant. Electricity leapt in her nerves. Did the constable suspect something of the relationship developing between her and Max? She was beginning to think that behind PC Cheney's bluff, somewhat clumsy, exterior there was a sharp and intuitive intellect at work.

She smiled at him, raising her eyebrows in a silent question. *Is he here yet?* On no account would she allow her eyes to stray to the table where Max had been sitting the previous evening with Emma Hayes.

The constable nodded towards the bar, indicating with his eyes a stocky man with a swarthy face and close cropped hair who was sitting staring into his glass of wine and giving off signals of being deeply uncomfortable.

PC Cheney turned back to Isabel and, with a jolt, she registered that once again his glance into her face was just a fraction longer than necessary, that there was a thoughtful glaze of speculation in his eyes as they met hers. The notion that he might have some evidence of her closeness with Max set her arteries jangling.

She took a breath, lifted her head and gave him a nod of gracious acknowledgement as he took her cape to hang it up.

Walking up to the stocky, uneasy man waiting at the bar, she spoke in a low, shy voice. 'Mr Montague?' she queried.

He looked up. He had the blunt squashed features of a boxer. He was certainly not at all good-looking but he had very clear blue eyes and his smile seemed genuine. 'Miss Bruce?'

She smiled. 'Isabel.'

'Call me Jim.' He cleared his throat, seeming uncertain what to say next. 'Can I order you a drink?' he managed eventually.

They ordered their food and were shown to their table where they ate their way solemnly, and mostly in silence, through a starter and a main course. Isabel found she had to make all the conversational running. James Montague was gauche and unsure of himself – ill at ease and painfully shy. But he was pleasant enough and he didn't boast or try to patronise her the way Jeremy had done.

Was this a man who could set out to terrorise women? she wondered. Was this *the* man? Was his shyness inadequacy? Or was it some kind of devious smoke screen he was putting up in order to hide himself? Was he feigning uncertainty to get her do all the talking and make her reveal things about herself whilst he maintained his secrecy? She had no idea what the answer was. It seemed an impossible task even to make a guess.

She glanced across to Max. Once again, he and Emma were playing the part of a loving couple, leaning across the table and looking into each other's eyes. Tonight Emma was wearing emerald green. Her shoulders were bare, the skin gleaming and faintly tanned. Her hair fell around her face in a heavy shiny curtain. She looked very attractive indeed and a tiny bolt of jealousy jumped through Isabel's taut nerves.

She and Jim had now progressed to the pudding. Isabel had tried her best to draw him out by telling him one or two of her own secrets. Of the loneliness of being a woman new to London, about her occasional fears for her safety. She went so far as to mention accounts she had seen in the papers of women who had been stalked or mugged.

Jim listened gravely and attentively, nodding in agreement with whatever views she expressed. He offered nothing of his own in return.

Before the coffee arrived, Isabel made her way to the cloakroom. In the privacy of one of the scented cubicles, she took a tiny notepad from her bag, tore off a sheet of paper and wrote: 'Don't think this is our man. Sorry, can't be more specific.'

Emma was waiting beside the basins, washing her hands. Another woman stood beside the large illuminated mirror in the corner of the room re-touching her make-up. Isabel washed her hands, dried them on a tissue and slid the note to Emma who read it and slipped it into her minuscule evening bag. She gave a brief impersonal smile to Isabel, but it was long enough for Isabel to spot that tiny razor-like glint of speculation she had seen in Jack Cheney's expression earlier. Then she quietly left the room.

Isabel dabbed some perfume onto her wrists. She knew that each of the men involved in this flushing-out exercise would be followed when they left the restaurant as a matter of routine. There was no question of any of them vanishing into the darkness of the London streets. They would be carefully tracked until they reached their next destination, or the place they were to spend the night.

And yet, she still had a sense of failure. She wanted to help catch this man who was making innocent women's life a misery. And she wanted desperately to help Max – she knew how important this case was to him. Somehow she felt she should have been able to do better. Spot something about Jim's personality that would give Max and his team something to work on.

Jim was stirring his coffee thoughtfully as she sat down at the table once again. 'I've got something to tell you,' he said abruptly.

Oh God! Not another cheating husband Isabel thought.

'I answered your advert because I needed someone to take to a family wedding. I've never had much luck with women and my cousin bet me £1,000 I wouldn't be able to pull a really gorgeous, cultured red-head to take along as my girlfriend.'

Isabel gaped at him and then burst out laughing.

'It's not really the money I'm worried about' he said

ruefully. I've been away for the last year working on an oil rig in the North Sea. I'm loaded with cash, as a matter of fact.'

'It's a question of masculine pride?' Isabel suggested.

'Yeah. But you see...' He stopped, his cheeks flushing dark red. 'I've already got someone to fill the bill. I answered two adverts, and I met this girl last night and she thought it was all a real laugh. She rang just before I set off here and said she was definitely up for it.'

'You're telling me I'm surplus to requirements?' Isabel asked, her lips twitching.

'Yeah, I'm sorry. It was too late to let you know and I didn't want to stand you up. I'm really very sorry.'

'No need,' Isabel reassured him. 'I wouldn't have been "up for it" anyway. Acting a part isn't really my favourite activity!'

Jim insisted on buying her brandy to drink with her coffee and then paying the bill. They parted amicably at the bottom of the iron staircase.

Isabel's 'taxi' was already waiting and she jumped quickly into it, instructing the driver to take her straight home. There was nothing she would have wanted more than to linger until Max came to join her, which she knew he would in a minute or so. And there was nothing she considered more dangerous, now being uncomfortably apprehensive that both Emma Hayes and Jack Cheneys' suspicions about her and Max had been aroused.

Max telephoned her soon after she arrived back at her flat. He was at his most distant and formal and she guessed he was back at the station, and that Emma and Jack were hovering around, ears twitching.

'You put on a splendid show!' he commented. 'How did things go?'

Isabel gave a brief resume. 'I'm pretty sure Jim Gaunt's not the Batterer,' she concluded. 'From what I could gather he's been on an oil rig in the North Sea until a few days ago.'

'Right. We'll check on that.' There was a pause. 'What about tomorrow? This next guy on the list, Kelvin Gaunt? Do you feel up to going through with another meeting?'

'I don't seem to be having much luck with the "dates" you've fixed for me so far,' she remarked, partly-rueful, partly-joking.

'I don't need reminding of that,' he said tersely.

'My experiences to date certainly don't encourage me to go looking for a man in the lonely hearts columns,' she said, unable to resist teasing him.

'I should hope not.' Another pause. 'Isabel, be honest. Are you sure you want to go ahead with Gaunt?'

'Of course. Maybe we'll hit the jackpot this time.'

'We can but hope,' he agreed.

Kelvin Gaunt was the youngest of the three men Isabel had telephoned in order to arrange a meeting.

He was waiting for her just inside the door of the restaurant. 'Hello Isabel?' he said hesitantly, holding out his hand.

'Hello Kelvin.' She smiled at him. This evening she wore a silver velvet suit. There was no need for her cape and Jack Cheney was denied the job of rushing forward to take it from her.

'Do you mind if we go straight to the table?' Kelvin asked with a hint of apology. 'I'm rather hungry. Haven't eaten all day.'

'Fine!' She followed him through the restaurant, noting that Max and Emma were already in their usual places.

They sat down and Kelvin absorbed himself in the menu. He was tall and slim with boyish good looks and had pale smooth skin and light-brown hair that reached to the tips of his ears. It was obviously freshly washed and swung to and fro as he moved his head. He wore a very white T-shirt and a stylishly-creased linen jacket.

After they had ordered the food, he leaned forward and began to ask Isabel all about herself. He asked about her family, where she had been to school, her student days and, finally, her current job. She noticed that he listened carefully to all her answers, as though they were magnetically interesting. Or as if he was storing them up to run through again later.

'You're the head of a financial department!' he exclaimed. 'That's amazing!'

'Why?' She waited for the inevitable male response – 'You're far too pretty,' or some such sexist comment.

'Oh, I don't know. I admire anyone who can understand accounts and that sort of thing. I'm useless.'

Isabel found herself charmed. 'So what do you do?'

'Computer stuff. Fixing them when they go wrong.'

'Even more amazing!' she smiled. 'I just swear at mine and hit it when it won't work. It doesn't do the slightest good.'

He smiled. His eyes were bright and alive and there was a restless energy about him. He really was very attractive. And he hadn't made one single personal comment on her appearance or her red hair. Thank goodness!

It can't be him, she thought, hating even to think such a thought.

And then she sternly reminded herself that of course it could be him. Anyone was suspect. But not him, surely.

The first course arrived. PC Cheney glided up and

poured wine. Very expertly. Isabel murmured thanks, then looked across the table and saw Kelvin eagerly examining his grilled sardines and sautéed potatoes. He glanced up and gave her a beautiful smile. He seemed to be so happy and excited at the prospect of his food and the rest of their evening together. His anticipation was like a light shining behind his eyes.

As the meal drew to its close, Kelvin summoned a passing waiter and asked for the bill. Isabel sipped her coffee and it was at this point she realised that she had been so relaxed and well-entertained by Kelvin, that she had omitted to turn up for her meeting in the cloakroom with Emma Hayes! She was just about to right the error when the waiter turned up with the itemised bill.

'Let me go halves,' she said to Kelvin, picking up her bag.

'No, please. I want to pay. Truly.' He started rooting in his pockets. 'Oh, hell! Where have I put the cash?' He blushed like a schoolboy.

'I'll come back in a moment, Sir,' the waiter said tactfully, walking away.

'Oh! Thank goodness, it's here.' Kelvin pulled a roll of notes from the pocket of his combat-style trousers. With the money came a flash of silver and there was the clink of metal on the woodblock floor. Isabel looked down and saw four chunky rings rolling at random, scattering and then settling into stillness. They were substantial items of jewellery, adorned with heavily-spiked faces like gargoyles. She stared at them fascinated.

Kelvin grinned and swiftly bent to scoop them up, sliding them back into his pocket.

At that moment, Isabel jerked into an altered state of awareness. It was as though she had been in a mist and, quite suddenly, the clouds had lifted and she could see all around. Everything was crystal clear, like a landscape defined against a cold blue sky. There was no doubt in her mind. She had never forgotten Max's voice as he quietly told her what The Batterer did to his victims. He crept up on them from behind and overpowered them. And when they were too weak and terrified to fight back, he beat their faces to a pulp.

She could see it now, Kelvin's eyes luminous with excitement as he laid into his victims with only his hand for a weapon. But a hand armed with four punishing, damaging rings!

What now? What now? she asked herself, her heart racing in panic and agitation.

'Where do you live?' Kelvin was saying, smiling at her with sunny appeal.

'About ten minutes away.'

'I'll walk you home. If that's all right by you,' he added hastily.

'I've got a taxi booked,' she flashed back. It would be so easy to get away from him, she thought. But then, supposing Max and Emma tracked him back to his home but couldn't find any hard evidence, could build no case against him. Had he left any traces on his victims? Anything the forensic department could use to match for DNA? She couldn't remember Max having said anything about body traces being found. Maybe Kelvin was really clever. Maybe when he was out on the prowl he wore a hat to keep his hair secure. Maybe he wore surgical gloves to do his cruel beating work.

Her heart thundered and her fingers clenched, the nails biting into the flesh of her palms. She knew she could not walk away from this. She had to get some evidence to use against Kelvin, some concrete proof of his brutality and cunning. She had to help Max nail this monster who posed as a shy charmer.

'Oh.' He looked crestfallen.

'You could come back with me,' she heard herself say. Good God, had she gone completely mad? 'Back to my place.' Now she was playing the seductress. Oh Heavens!

'Hey, that would be great. But are you sure?' he wondered, his eyes shining with concern. 'You don't know anything about me, you've only just met me...'

'Oh, I'm sure,' she said faintly, hearing her voice as if it were coming through some kind of muffling gauze.

'Well then!' he said, jumping up. 'Let's go.' He counted out several notes and laid them on the table, carefully placing a plate on top to keep them secure.

Placing his hand lightly on Isabel's arm, he propelled her to the door. She could sense his intense excitement, his tingling anticipation of what was to come. They walked down the iron staircase together. She noticed that Kelvin's hold on her arm had tightened. His fingers around her muscles were like a restraint of steel.

Isabel looked around in panic for *her* taxi. Where was it? Come on, come on! At least in the police vehicle she would have some protection, and time to think what she must do next. Another cab drew up, a standard black London cab with its yellow light switched on, showing it was free.

Kelvin raised his arm and the taxi drew into the kerb. Isabel felt herself propelled towards it, felt her body freeze with fear.

And then there was a voice behind her shouting her name. She was pushed roughly away from the open door of taxi, almost falling to the pavement as she lost her footing and stumbled.

A tall figure cannoned against her, then streaked away into the darkness. Another figure followed, his legs going like pistons. Isabel shook her head as though to clear the fog that swirled in her brain. It seemed all this had happened in no more than a couple of seconds.

As clear thinking returned, she found herself standing in the cold street, her arm firmly held by Emma Hayes.

'Are you OK?' Emma asked her.

'Yes.' She looked around. She saw that the black taxi cab had moved away. Her own police 'taxi' stood at the kerb, its back door open.

'Get in,' Emma instructed her. On a reflex, Isabel moved forward obediently then stopped. 'Where's Max?'

'Chasing after Gaunt. Get in the taxi, Isabel,' Emma insisted.

They drove through the streets. Isabel put up a hand to push her hair from her face. Her fingers shook so violently she soon abandoned any attempt to tidy herself up and replaced her hands in her lap.

'What was going on back there?' Emma asked, her tone calm and even, but Isabel could feel the tension and anger behind the other woman's voice.

'It was him. The monster, The Batterer.'

'How did you know?'

'I just knew. He had these rings. Great big ugly ones like armour. And he was so alive, so excited. He was like an animal hunting his prey, closing in for the kill.'

She thought she heard Emma sigh. 'What were you thinking of going off with him on your own?' the woman asked.

'I wanted to get some evidence. So you could make a case against him.'

Another sigh.

'All right,' Isabel agreed, 'I know it sounds emotional and silly, a truly crazy thing to do. But somehow I was compelled to do it.'

'You could have got yourself into a very difficult situation,' Emma pointed out. 'The police would have been responsible. Inspector Hawthorne would have been put on the line.'

Isabel winced. 'Oh for God's sake,' she flashed back. 'Use your imagination, Emma. People under pressure, even quite sane ones, sometimes act on impulse. You might even try it yourself one day.'

Emma gave a little cough. After a short, prickly silence Emma's mobile rang. 'Sergeant Hayes,' she answered crisply. There was a long pause. 'I see, sir,' said Emma. Another pause. 'Right then, sir. Goodnight.'

'Well? Isabel prompted urgently.

'That was Inspector Hawthorne. He and Constable Cheney are with Gaunt at his flat. They've found photographs of the two girls Gaunt beat-up and strands of their hair. Also, one of the girl's scarves with her blood on it. And besides the rings, he had a very sharp knife and a long piece of wire in his pockets this evening.'

Relief flowed through Isabel like a warm stream. 'Is that enough to put him in court?' she asked.

'Oh, yes.'

'Yes!' exclaimed the officer driving the car, thumping the wheel in triumph.

'Inspector Hawthorne was very pleased,' Emma told Isabel formally. 'He asked me to thank you for all your co-operation in helping us bring this criminal to justice.'

'Yes,' Isabel acknowledged softly. She felt as though her life had been given back to her. She could walk alone in the streets without looking back all the time. She could sleep in her bed, not lie in the darkness, listening, waiting. She could say good-bye to fear.

And very soon she and Max could begin a life together.

chapter fourteen

After a long, untroubled sleep, Isabel woke refreshed and filled with energy. She got up at seven and made herself a jug of good, strong coffee. Then she baked a chocolate cake because she suddenly felt very female and creative.

She went out into the High Street when the shops opened and bought an armful of white Longi lilies, from the local flower stall.

Walking back to her flat, she smiled to note the absence of the police car which had become a fixture in the past weeks, the constant stream of officers watching her house.

She noticed the children from the house opposite walking down the street on the opposite pavement – Flo's former tormentors. She supposed they would be setting out for school. One of them gave her a tentative wave and she waved gaily back, feeling in tune with all the world this morning.

Leaving the lilies in the sink to have a good drink of cold water, she telephoned Esther at the office. 'I'm thinking of taking the day off,' she told her cheerily.

'Wow!' said Esther. 'Never known before in the whole history of your working life!'

'Probably not,' Isabel agreed. 'What's in my diary for today?'

There was the sound of flicking of pages. Managers' meeting in the conference room all day. Lunch booked for midday at the bistro round the corner.'

Isabel smiled. 'That means we won't see any of the partners back until four o'clock, and then they'll most likely fall asleep from having too much wine.'

'I think you can safely miss all of it,' Esther said. 'And hey, when I think of all the overtime you've done since I started working for you, I think you have a solemn duty to take the day off and enjoy yourself.'

'Thanks Esther. But give me a call if anything urgent comes up, or if there are any queries from individual clients.'

'Sure. But it'll have to be very urgent indeed before I bother you. Have a super, super day!'

Isabel drifted about, enjoying her freedom, carrying out little tasks to make her flat look loved and lived-in once more. She polished her dining-table with beeswax, then plumped up the cushions from the sofa in the sitting-room. Having arranged the lilies in a tall glass vase she placed them centrally on the table. Already their sweet exotic fragrance was perfuming the air.

Just after eleven o'clock, she saw Max's tall figure coming down her steps. Rushing to the door she flung it open, and pulled him inside.

He kissed her, holding her so hard against him she thought he would crush every one of her ribs.

'You look terrible,' she exclaimed when eventually she pulled herself away from him. 'How long is it since you slept?'

'I can't remember.' He looked dazed with fatigue, on the point of collapse. Isabel led him into her bedroom and pushed him gently down on the bed. 'Close your eyes,' told him softly. She sat beside him, rhythmically stroking his thick hair until his breathing deepened and his eyelids closed. He slept but only for half an hour. When he woke, he looked up at her, his face stern, his eyes intense with speculation.

'Please don't ask me what the hell I was thinking of to put myself at risk with that dreadful man last night,' she said, guessing at his thoughts.

'Do you really see me in the role of the stern headmaster quizzing the wayward pupil?' he asked.

'Your sergeant made a very good job of playing the headmistress,' Isabel observed.

Max gave a wry smile. 'I *was* angry with you, just for a moment,' he admitted. 'Furious that you suddenly lost the script and started acting out of character.'

'It was like a compulsion bubbling up inside me,' she said, frowning as she tried to recapture the sensation. 'I suddenly knew Kelvin Gaunt was the man you and your team had been looking for. The man who tortured women.'

Max nodded, watching her carefully. He always made her feel that no one had ever looked at her properly before. 'And you wanted to make absolutely sure he didn't go free, didn't you? It felt like a personal responsibility, a mission. Even though you knew we had everything in place to get him if there was the remotest shred of evidence?'

She touched the dark crescents of weariness under his eyes with tender fingers. 'Yes,' she said slowly. 'That's exactly what was going on in my head. How did you know?'

'I read minds,' he said with a grim smile. 'It's what we're paid to do in the police.'

'I'm sorry I gave you those few moments from hell, Max,' she whispered.

'I should hope so. Don't ever, ever do it again.'

She rolled herself on top of him. The stubble on his chin grazed her face as they kissed. 'I have to get back to work,' he groaned.

'I know. Will you come to Edinburgh with me for a day or two? I need to see my father. He's not very well at the moment, and I'd like to introduce you to each other.'

His face took on a thoughtful expression, as he swung his legs down to the floor and stood up.

'Well?' she prompted.

'Yes,' he said, his voice low. 'I'd like that very much.'

'Is it still risky?' she wondered, concerned to hear the caution in his voice. 'Our being together?'

'Not really. And I'd very much like to meet your father.' He went to the mirror and raked his hands through his hair, straightened the collar of his shirt.

'I'm sorry Max, I didn't realise I was asking you to do something you don't feel comfortable with,' she said. 'I thought now the case was sewn up...'

'You will almost certainly be called as a witness at Gaunt's – or should I say Trevor Williams' – trial,' he explained, undoing his tie and then re-knotting it. 'Which technically means that if our affair became public, we could be liable to some questions from the court. They'd most likely take a dim view of a key police officer for the prosecution consorting with a witness.'

'Oh dear!' she said, suddenly understanding.

He turned and took her hands in his. 'Don't look so dismayed. The main evidence of this case will be based on forensic information and the accounts of the two women who were injured. You won't be a key witness. So, as long as we're careful, I don't think we need worry too much.' He smiled and kissed her very gently.

'I am worried!' she exclaimed. 'I wouldn't do anything

to harm your career. You know that, Max. I'm prepared to wait until the trial's over…'

'Are you, my love?' he said with steely softness. 'I'm not. And come hell or high water, I'll get myself some leave arranged. We'll go away together. We'll be miles away from London and all the circumstances of this grim case. God!' he exclaimed, pushing his hands through his hair, 'I've waited long enough for a shred of happiness to seep back into my life. I'm not going to throw it away now.'

Isabel put her arms around him and held him close. She understood that since his wife's death he had been lonely and troubled. With a strange mixture of compassion and arrogance, he had set himself apart from his fellow human beings and worked single-mindedly to try to right the wrongs of a cruel, heartless world. He had ignored his own needs and emotions and let his heart become a cold, frozen organ. And now that it was thawing out, he was uncertain, seeing horizons which had been hidden for far too long.

I shall take such good care of you, my wonderful Max, she thought as she rubbed her hands across the bones of his shoulders and his back. 'Go now,' she whispered. 'Go back to your work and the people who rely on you. They need you.'

When he had gone, she telephoned the hospital and was reassured that her father was well and in good spirits. They couldn't give her any further details at this point, all they could say was that there was no cause for alarm.

Isabel sat on her sofa and indulged in the luxury of filling her mind with thoughts of Max. She had always been rather steady, not given to impulse, not given to falling wildly in love – unlike Luisa who had been quite the opposite. Still was! Yet now she felt changed. It was as though she had been a rock and suddenly a great wave had bowled her over, had bruised and buffeted her until she felt the very edges of her soul had been subtly refashioned.

'Oh Max,' she groaned into the empty room.

Max slotted himself into the chair behind his desk and stared at his computer. He pressed three keys and Trevor Williams' past record sprang onto the screen. Not much to speak of. A couple of petty thefts from shops when he was in his teens, a speeding offence whilst driving his father's Jaguar, a caution for harassing a female neighbour two years before, but no charges brought. Hardly surprising their computer search details had failed to come up with his name.

The elation of Williams' arrest ebbed and flowed within him like a tide. Max was one hundred percent convinced of Gaunt's guilt. They had caught the right man for the appropriate offences.

But there was a new theory developing. A fear that nagged at him, aching like a troublesome tooth. And Isabel's continued safety was at the heart of that fear. Isabel, his new and precious love. But there was nothing he could do about the suspicion gripping him. Except wait.

chapter fifteen

They took a flight to Glasgow, where Max picked up a hire car to drive them out to the Highlands.

Isabel's father had telephoned to let her know he was pleased by the results of his medical tests, and also to tell her that on his discharge from hospital, he had decided to leave the bustle of Edinburgh and decamp to his holiday house on the west coast for a few days.

'Recuperation and celebration, my dear,' he told her. 'That's what I need. I shall be delighted to see you and, of course, your gentleman friend. We shall take walks by the lochs and sit beside log fires in the evenings.'

Isabel, sitting in the passenger seat and contemplating her father's reaction to her new 'friend', kept sneaking glances at Max's hawk-like profile as he concentrated on negotiating the car along the narrow, undulating roads. She found it hard to believe they were really here, deep in the Scottish countryside, and at last alone together. The sensation was unreal and suffused with magic.

The light was fading as they turned on to the road leading north out of Lochgilphead, snaking its way along the line of the coast. Little pinpoints of light showed in the villages beside the road and, beyond them, she could see the electric-blue reflection of Loch Melfort, it's gleaming water enclosed between the dark masses of the hills. Looking inland, she glimpsed streaks of tumbling white waters, streams rushing down from the mountain forests in a furious roaring torrent. When she opened the car window she could taste the spray.

'Have you been here before?' she asked Max.

'No. It's awesome. Unique.'

She smiled. 'Look, an owl!' she exclaimed as a grey shape flitted silently across the view, then turned in the air and zoomed away, heading for the dark forest. They heard the soft echo of its hoot from the shelter of the trees. Isabel took a deep breath that tasted of rain and wind and the sweet sharpness of pine resin. 'Aah,' she sighed, leaning her head back and swivelling it towards Max, her lips curving in a smile of pure love.

Alastair Bruce's country retreat stood at the head of Loch Melfort looking out towards the Western Isles. It was a solid, square house standing on its own, built of grey stone with pointed candle-snuffer turrets at each of its four corners.

As Max drew the car to a halt on the driveway he imagined himself visiting such a house in the course of his work, standing at the front door with his hand on the knocker, anticipating an interview with a witness or a suspect. It struck him that his first thought would have been that a country residence as substantial as this, represented considerable wealth. And that wealth had a habit of creating discord and jealousy.

As it turned out, there was no question of standing at the door knocking; the arched oak front door stood wide open in welcome. As Isabel and Max stepped from the car, stretching themselves after the long drive, a neat bird-like woman with silver hair cut in a short page-boy bob came out to greet them.

'Isabel! My dear. So lovely to see you again. Come away in!'

Max glanced around the impressive hallway, swiftly taking in its graceful symmetrical proportions, the white-painted walls and the central staircase of pale oak with it ruby-red carpet. Huge canvases supported by chains hung from the dado rail. Their colours were subdued and stormy, depicting rainswept moors presided over by stags with huge, intricate antlers. A log fire crackled in a stone fireplace set in a deep alcove. Everything gleamed and there was a fragrance of woodsmoke and beeswax.

Mrs Pringle led them into an oak-panelled room. There were shelves with leather-bound books lined up along one wall and yet another open fire, this one blazing energetically in a heavy iron dog grate.

He watched Isabel walk around to the front of a high-backed leather armchair drawn up to the fire and smile down hesitantly at the occupant, who was as yet invisible from where Max stood.

'Father,' she said gently, and Max felt there was some kind of question in her voice.

'My dear, how good to see you.' The voice was silvery and cultured, full of paternal authority.

She bent to kiss him. 'How are you? You said you were pleased with the results of the tests?'

'Perfectly satisfied, just what I had expected. Nothing for everyone to get excited about. Now where is this gentleman friend of yours, hmm?'

Isabel made a little gesture and Max stepped forward. Standing close to Isabel, he extended his hand to the aristocratic, but very frail-looking, man who sat in the chair. Looking at the seventy year old Alastair Bruce, Max could see from whom Isabel had inherited her delicate, carved bone structure. Her father's skin might be pale and papery, and the flesh hanging in folds around his neck, lizard-like and ugly, but however ill he might or might not be, either now or in the future, he would never lose his elegant looks. The fine fretwork of his bones would see to that.

'Ah, Inspector Hawthorne,' Alastair Bruce said with an almost regal formality. 'Isabel has told me very little about you. But no doubt we shall find out more in due course. We're very pleased to welcome you to our home. Do please make yourself comfortable.' He gestured to a fat leather chair on the other side of the fire.

'Would you be taking a little whisky before dinner?' Mrs Pringle enquired, stepping forward and tweaking the tartan rug which was wrapped around her employer's thin legs.

'Thank you, yes,' Max said smiling.

'We have several Highland malts. Or maybe you'd like a blended whisky. There's a very fine one in the cabinet, which has been Mr Bruce's favourite for more years than I care to remember.'

'I'll have the blended,' Max said, thinking that this was going to be an interesting visit, although probably not at all relaxing.

'And a glass of Chablis for you, dear?' Mrs Pringle wondered, smiling fondly at Isabel who was perched, somewhat uneasily in Max's view, on a fat leather stool beside her father's chair. 'I brought some from the cellar of the Edinburgh house specially for you.'

'Thank you,' Isabel smiled. Max wondered if Isabel would have preferred whisky and what Mrs Pringle's reaction would have been if she had told her so!

He recalled Isabel's telling him on their first meeting that her mother had died when she was just ten years old. He had a new and vivid image of Isabel as a girl, growing into womanhood, lonely and motherless. He pictured what it would have been like for her living in a draughty Edinburgh house with her patrician, distant father and the amiable, but controlling Mrs Pringle.

They sipped their drinks and then progressed into the dining-room where the long, oval table was formally set with glinting silver and glassware. Yet another fire burned in a splendid mahogany fireplace with a high mantelpiece. Which was just as well, Max thought, as the place obviously had no other heating and the far corners of the rooms were freezing cold.

Mrs Pringle brought in soup and warmed floury baps. 'I've got a wee girl from the village helping out in the kitchen,' she told Isabel confidentially. 'Your father says I'm getting too old to do the cooking *and* the washing up.'

'We are none of us getting any younger,' Mr Bruce observed, smiling at his housekeeper and making Max wonder if the two of them had some kind of 'arrangement'. He decided not. They belonged to another world, another generation from the permissive present. He saw them perfectly fitting the old traditional roles of respected employer, and loyal retainer who loved every minute of her job.

'You're looking rather strained, my dear,' Mr Bruce observed, peering at Isabel and frowning. 'Have you been working too hard?'

'Probably,' Isabel said casually. 'Everyone in the finance business works too hard, Father. It's considered normal.' There was the faintest hint of challenge in her voice.

Max found himself intrigued by the relationship between father and daughter. He had seen Isabel upset and living on her nerves through constant fear, but he had never seen her as she was with her father. On the surface she was the loving and confident daughter, but underneath he sensed that she was ill-at-ease, worried about his reaction to each sentence she uttered, painfully anxious to please him. Yet at the same time, she was determined to be true to herself and express her own views. He guessed it would have been a major decision to invite him, Max, to this fortress to meet her father.

Alastair Bruce was the sort of man who could easily take against a stranger, especially one outside his own privileged world, and a man who looked likely to be a part of his daughter's future.

He had already noticed how Mr Bruce brushed aside all Isabel's attempts to persuade him to offer details about his recent hospital visit. He simply repeated his satisfaction at having been given a clean bill of health as he termed it. Max wondered what he was hiding, and what Isabel's thoughts on the subject were.

The meal was excellently cooked, although the roast Aberdeen Angus beef and accompanying vegetables were almost cold. It was clearly a very difficult task to keep food hot on the way from the kitchen, which Max guessed would be north facing and as cold as the Arctic!

'Are the police improving their record on catching criminals?' Mr Bruce asked Max, fixing him with his vivid blue eyes. 'We seem to hear fluctuating reports.'

'Statistics should always to be treated with caution,' Max responded blandly.

'Mmm. And what are your prospects of becoming a Chief Inspector?' Mr Bruce demanded, making Isabel wince visibly.

'Quite good,' Max said evenly.

'I'm pleased to hear it. Especially as I have the impression my daughter is rather smitten with you, Inspector

Hawthorne. A state of affairs which does not come about very often, I might add.'

'Father!' Isabel protested.

'I believe in speaking my mind, my dear,' her father told her mildly. 'Any man who looks likely to share your future deserves such frankness, don't you think?' The blue eyes pierced Max.

'Yes, I do. And I shall take very good care of her, Mr Bruce,' Max said in low even tones.

'I'm pleased to hear it. But as far as money is concerned, I don't really need to ask about your prospects, young man. I had a very lucrative career following my father into his ship-building business. Isabel will inherit more than enough from me to keep herself and her family in comfort for the rest of their lives. All I need to know about you is that you are not a bounder and a wastrel who will squander her fortune. And from what I've seen of you, I'm quite satisfied. Now if you will excuse me,' he said, rising to his feet, 'I think it is time I should retire.'

As if by magic, Mrs Pringle glided in, whipped up her employer's tartan rug which had fallen on the floor, draped it around his shoulders and gently propelled him from the room.

'Oh God!' groaned Isabel, dropping her head into her hands.

Max went to sit beside her, put his arms around her and kissed her cheek softly. 'I appear to have been put to the test and awarded a marginal pass.'

'I should have warned you,' she said ruefully. 'He's really a darling, but he has no truck with small talk. And he can be rather…blunt.'

'He likes to get straight to the heart of the matter?'

'Yes. Oh dear. And all that Jane Austen stuff about "prospects" and "fortunes" and the future. He can be overly blunt and direct.'

'He doesn't bother shooting darts unless he's going to hit the bull's-eye,' Max suggested with irony. 'Don't worry I can take it. Compared with some of the people I have to question, your father is a cuddly pussy cat.' He stroked the back of her neck with gentle, tender fingers. 'Besides which, I rather thought we both had prospects – for a long and loving future.'

She turned to look into his face. His lips pressed on hers and for some time there was no more discussion, just a long, pulsing, delicious silence.

Later on, they made love in a freezing cold bedroom snuggled beneath a huge feathery duvet.

'I thought we might have been banished to separate rooms,' Max murmured with irony, leaning up on his elbow and stroking her cheek. 'And that Mrs Pringle would have been patrolling the dark corridors in her night-gown, holding a candle, all ready to pounce if she caught me sneaking along for a secret rendezvous in the sanctum of your maidenly chamber.'

'I don't think either she or my father are quite as far back in history as that,' Isabel chuckled.

She felt filled with joy. It was as though she were at the start of some wonderful journey. Max and she would embark on a new life together, and with him she would discover things she hadn't even begun to imagine before.

The horror of the past few weeks when she had lived in a dark cage of fear was all falling away from her, melting in the heat of Max's tenderness towards her and the passion of his love-making.

Lying in Max's arms and gazing into his dark, warrior-like face made her suddenly understand why people did the craziest, most out of character things for love. She had always held rather firm views on the benefits of a steady, ordered life. She supposed she had learned that from her father. But now she felt a new sympathy for those people who suddenly gave themselves up to passion; who would abandon the reassuring routine of their worthy lives, would throw up their careers, or even start wars in order to be with their loved one.

It was the same for Max. When he made love to Isabel and held her close to him, he felt a surging new hope for the future. The years of bleak loneliness, nights when he had lain awake tortured with thoughts of his dead wife. Friends and colleagues told him that time heals grief. But whilst the agony of his sorrow eventually became blunted, he found that every day he woke with a sense of sadness, feeling that Jenny was moving further and further away from him into the past. That the distance between them was growing with each month and year that went by. He tried to bring her back through his memory, but her features were indistinct; it was only in dreams that he saw them exactly and the next day, the reality of her death would sweep over him all over again, leaving him to battle against a fresh sense of loss.

But now with Isabel he was learning how to let the past go. When he looked into her beautiful, luminous eyes he saw a mirror image of the love that was welling up inside him. It fuelled him with desire, but at the same time filled him with a blissful sense of contentment which had been missing from his life for so long.

They only had a short time to stay in the Highlands. The time went swiftly, partly because of the strict routine of the house which was born of long habit – rituals which

Isabel remembered from her childhood and which both she and Max found curiously reassuring.

Breakfast for the two of them at eight-thirty, then a long walk through the forests or by the shores of Loch Melfort. Then back to the house, by which time Mr Bruce would be up and about and Mrs Pringle would be busy pouring tiny glasses of dry sherry before lunch. In the afternoons, they went out in Mr Bruce's splendid 1971 two-litre Rover. Max took the wheel and drove wherever the older man guided him. They drove through Glen Coe, grim and magnificent under the slate-grey clouds, then made their way back through the Glen of Orchy, where the river hurled itself between its banks like a roaring black monster.

There would be tea and buttered scones and cherry cake waiting when they got back and they would sit by the fire, listening to Mr Bruce's reflections on recent political developments and discussing the ins-and-outs of modern policing with Max.

After that, Isabel would insist on helping Mrs Pringle wash the dishes, before going up to the arctic bedroom and shivering as she changed for dinner, knowing how much her father liked the observation of form and style.

'Why didn't you tell me to bring a dinner jacket?' Max teased, surveying his informal slacks and black leather jacket in the mirror. 'Thank goodness I had the foresight to pack a tie.'

'Oh Father keeps a supply of suitable ties for guests who have forgotten about gracious living,' Isabel laughed. 'So you wouldn't have been thrown out.' She glanced at him in sudden anxiety. 'I know Father's a bit of a stickler for formalities. Are you finding it tiresome?'

He strode across the room and hugged her against him.

'I'm having the time of my life,' he said bending to kiss her. 'I wouldn't want to change a thing.'

Buoyed up with her new freedom from harassment and fear, but mostly by this wonderful new sense of being loved by a man whom she felt she could die for, Isabel found the courage to talk to her father about Luisa before she and Max set off back to London. To talk far more frankly than she had ever dared before.

She began by filling him in on Luisa's plans to appear in the TV thriller, and then told him a little about Josh and how pleasant he seemed. How happy the two of them seemed together.

Her father listened with polite attentiveness, but she could sense his scepticism. Like Max, he had a disconcerting way of making you feel he could see quite clearly into your thoughts and motivations.

'You see, Father,' she concluded, 'the simple truth is it makes me sad that you and she seem to be – how can I put it? – out of tune with each other.'

He sighed and frowned in consideration. 'I think that is a very good way of putting it,' he said slowly. 'How perceptive of you, my dear.'

'Yes, well, it's all very well agreeing with me,' Isabel protested. 'But I don't want you and Luisa to be like that.'

'What *do* you want, Isabel?'

'For you and Luisa to show some tolerance for each other. You're very different in temperament and outlook, but you're father and daughter.'

'You want us to play happy families – hmm?'

'I want us to *be* a happy family. After all, you and Luisa are my only family. You're very precious to me.'

Her father smiled. 'You are very like your mother,

Isabel; wise and also tender-hearted. But Luisa is much more like me, steely and iron-willed. I doubt that we have ever got on and now it's much too late.'

'No!'

Her father's face hardened. 'I had thought she would grow out of her waywardness and her promiscuity. Oh, call me old-fashioned, but the morals of the current generation appall me. And to sleep with men you hardly know and then become pregnant and get rid of the baby as though it were so much litter is utterly unpardonable.'

Suddenly Isabel understood the strength of his hostility towards his elder daughter. She shot a glance at him, did he know about Luisa's termination, or was he just speaking in general terms?

'How many abortions has she had?' he demanded, shuddering at the word. 'How many of her babies has she killed? Remind me.' His blue eyes bored into Isabel and she swallowed apprehensively, uncertain whether to tell the truth.

'One, that I am aware of,' he said flatly. 'Oh, I know all about this last one. She wanted a loan for the clinic fees. I had one or two very difficult calls from Australia once she discovered her condition.'

'You paid for her abortion?' Isabel was astounded.

'Oh yes. I've paid out some very considerable sums on Luisa's behalf over the years.'

'I thought she had a good income from her job. And...' Isabel stopped, thinking of the very generous trust-funds their father had set up for each of them on their twenty-first birthdays. Surely Isabel couldn't have spent all that.

'She is not like you, Isabel,' her father repeated quietly. 'You like to live within your means and to plan, whereas Luisa prefers to live in chaos. Well, I've made it rather plain to her that she is on her own from now on. I'm tired of being a bottomless well she can tap into whenever she runs short of ready cash.'

'Oh,' murmured Isabel, dismayed and at a loss.

Her father patted her hand. 'So, now might we talk of something different? Tell me about your plans for the future. I'd like you to know that I am most impressed by your friend Max Hawthorne. I may be getting old but I still pride myself on being a good judge of character and, in my view, he is a most excellent and worthy partner for you.'

'You approve?' Isabel queried, delighted.

'Indeed I do. So when he is going to make an honest woman of you – hmm?'

Later, just before they left for Glasgow to catch the evening flight back to London, she and Max walked into the forest behind the house and made their way along the broad stream that flowed in the valley. They held hands, their fingers occasionally tightening and then relaxing. Isabel lifted her face to the fresh breeze. Every nerve in her body seemed to tingle. Of one accord they stopped and stared into the silvery water, watching its glinting bubbles, the swoop and dip of the birds as they searched for fish.

'I love you my Isabel,' he said, touching her face with his fingers, exploring its soft contours. 'Will you stay with me, be mine? Always?'

'Yes,' she said. 'I'll always be yours.'

'Hey!' Esther exclaimed as Isabel walked in the next morning. 'Your little break up in the wilds has certainly done you good. You look all lit up.' She tilted her head on one side, considering. 'Radiant, that's the word!'

'I'm a new woman,' laughed Isabel. She looked at the pile of paperwork on her desk. 'Right!' she exclaimed, making a gesture of rolling up her sleeves. 'Let's get to work!'

At lunchtime she phoned Luisa, knowing that she would most likely only just have got out of bed. Actresses always seemed to be on late shifts, late nights and late mornings, even when they were not in a stage production. The habits learned in their early training in repertory theatre seemed to linger on.

'Izzie, darling! Are you OK?'

'Never better. And you? How's Josh?'

There was a tiny pause. 'He's fine, just fine.'

Somehow her brittle cheeriness was not reassuring. Isabel frowned, chewing her lip. 'I went up to see Father at the weekend.'

'Oh yes?'

'He seems fairly well, although he looks a lot older. But apparently the hospital tests were all negative.'

'Well, they would be wouldn't they?'

'What do you mean?'

'Even if they were dire he'd never admit it. I don't suppose you've actually spoken to his doctors.'

'Well no. He's perfectly capable of relaying the information himself.'

'Oh, yes. But maybe not the truth.'

'Look, Luisa, I'm not sure what you're getting at…'

'I'm sorry, sweetheart,' she said with genuine regret. 'Take no notice of me, I'm getting to be a suspicious, crabby bitch. I just think our parent is a wily old fox and as devious as hell. He'll tell us what he wants us to hear.'

'Yes, but that doesn't always exclude the truth.'

'No, of course it doesn't. I'm sure he's fine. Totally

indestructible, the obstinate old devil.'

'That's better!' Isabel laughed. 'Now when are we going to get together? You, me, Josh – and my new man.'

'Good Heavens!' exclaimed Luisa. 'That's the most fascinating news I've heard in ages. So that's why you were all glammed up the other evening. You wicked seductress, you!'

They parted with an agreement to consult their two men with a view to a dinner-date for four, later in the week.

When Isabel got back to her flat, late and happily tired that evening, she picked up her post and flicked through it. There was a brown envelope with a black rim. She stared at it and felt herself suddenly plunging back into a dark pit of fear.

She went into the kitchen, drew on some thin rubber gloves and took a small dessert knife from the cutlery drawer. With shaking hands she carefully slit open the envelope, easing the blade along the fold of the flap and taking great care not to make any actual contact with her fingers. But there were no hidden hazards. Just a single sheet of paper. The message was written in black capitals, with a thick felt-tip:

'HAVE YOU MISSED MY LETTERS ISABEL? DID YOU THINK IT WAS OVER BETWEEN US? THE THRILL OF PLEASURE AND PAIN? DON'T WORRY. WE WILL BE TOGETHER SOON. YOU WILL BE ALL MINE.'

She dropped the paper as though it were on fire. Then she phoned Max, but he was out seeing a witness. When the receptionist asked if there was an emergency, Isabel heard herself dully saying, 'No.' She felt too stunned to try to explain. She sat huddled in the corner of her sofa, her mind unable to focus on anything except the appalling thought that there was still someone out there who wanted to harm her. That nowhere was safe!

chapter sixteen

It was past two in the morning when Max arrived at Isabel's flat. He had spent the past few hours interviewing one of Trevor Williams/Kelvin Gaunt's victims. The young woman had previously been reluctant to speak about her ordeal, but then had suddenly changed her mind, and Max had thought it essential to see her before she changed it once again.

When he had accessed his voice-mail at the close of the interview he had driven straight to Isabel's flat, his face grim with anxiety, his worst fears aroused.

She was still dressed in her work clothes; a charcoal-grey suit with a pale, mint-green shirt. She looked pale and haunted and she looked as though someone had given her the kind of beating that crushes bones and bruises flesh, but doesn't show when you have all your clothes on. She looked as though she had already suffered the abuse she had been threatened with.

The note lay on the hall floor. He glanced swiftly at it and then took her into his arms, holding her in his loving protection, stroking her face and the soft skin of her neck under her hair. 'We'll get him,' he told her, feeling that the words, though heartfelt, were woefully inadequate.

'But what if he gets me first?'

Max winced. Dear God! 'He won't.'

'How can we be sure? Suppose I die when I'm not yet thirty? And forever after, people will remember me as poor, poor Isabel – the victim of a sadistic monster.'

He held her away from him and put his hands on her shoulders. 'Stop this! Don't let him win. Fight him, like you did before. Fight the evil and fight him. We'll step up the protection. He won't be able to get within yards of you and, before long, he'll get careless. He'll make a mistake and we'll have him.'

'I don't want to live in a cage,' she said with a pathos that tore at him. 'Not even a cage guarded by you.'

'I know, but what else can I do?'

'Nothing. You'll do all you can, I know that.' She looked up at him. 'And now we'll have to go back to keeping our love secret, won't we? Oh Max, I don't think I can bear it. God! This man knows how to torture me – torture us!'

'Yes,' Max said slowly, his mind automatically getting into gear, driving off down different avenues, forming theories. 'Would it make you feel any better if I asked to come off the case?'

'No!' she snapped back at him. 'Don't even think about it. I could never trust anyone but you to get this sadist.'

'Very well then. That's settled.' He pushed her down gently on to the sofa, then slid off her high-heeled shoes and rubbed her feet with tender fingers. He pulled her close and massaged the stretched wires of tension in her spine and at the base of her neck.

'What are we going to do?' she asked, her voice tearful. 'What happens now?'

'I shall arrange for a very close watch to be kept on the house. And with the help of my team, I shall trawl again through our computer records and see what we can come up with.'

'I see,' she said resignedly, sounding unconvinced.

'It's surprising how often dull routine methods throw

up results,' he told her. She nodded. It tore at his nerves to see her so inert, so defeated. 'Isabel, when I came to see you that very first time, I asked you about former boyfriends and about your family.'

'Yes. So?'

'You told me you had just had one significant relationship. I'd like you to tell me a bit more about that. About him.'

'Oh for goodness sake. You don't think it could be him who's doing this?'

'We can't rule anyone out,' he said patiently.

'Well, for what it's worth, his name is Andrew Yates and he's Dean of the Cathedral in a little town up in Yorkshire. Very highly-respected. He's married and I think he has two children. Pretty unlikely candidate, wouldn't you say?'

'Yes, but we'll check him out anyway. Don't worry, we'll be very discreet.'

'All right, go ahead,' said Isabel wearily. 'But it'll be a waste of time.'

'And what about your family? Is there anyone you haven't mentioned, besides your father and your half sister?'

'Oh God, now my Father's a suspect!'

'No, of course not.'

'I haven't any other family. I had two lovely eccentric aunts, my father's older sisters, but they died a few years ago.'

'Right.' Max wanted to ask more but he judged she was in no state for worrying and challenging questions.

'Do you think the letters and the parcel and the taxi and so on were all sent by the same person?' Isabel asked suddenly.

'You mean is it possible that Gaunt – sorry – Williams sent some of the things, at the same time as another man was targeting you?'

'Yes.' She winced at the horror of it – two separate pursuers.

'Williams certainly denies it. He claimed he'd never seen you or known anything about you before the night of the date.'

'Do you believe him?'

'Yes. I wasn't sure before, as you know. And we certainly have no tangible evidence against him as far as you were concerned.'

'Oh, how I hate all this.' She closed her eyes tight as though to shut all the horror out. 'It makes me feel somehow dirty. And sort of ashamed. Almost guilty myself.'

'No, that's nonsense.'

'You once said to me that in these sort of cases, you need to know as much as possible about the person who is the target. The personality of the victim holds some sort of key to the man targeting her. Don't you see Max, how that makes the victim feel? As though there's something wrong with *them*. I keep asking myself – "Why *me*?" What is it about me that attracted him? What's wrong with me that makes a weirdo or a madman so obsessed?'

'Yes, I understand,' he said slowly. 'But there isn't anything wrong with you, my darling. You're beautiful and desirable and intelligent and brave. And I love you so very much.'

'Well, you certainly know a good deal more than most people about me, Inspector,' she said with a faint, mocking smile. 'So you should have a head-start catching our man.'

They held each other in silence for a few moments.

'Find him, Max!' she pleaded urgently. 'Please find him…and quickly.'

Max sat in his office, staring at his computer screen with little sense of hope. He found himself adrift, a sailor on a rough sea in a paper canoe. The theory he had been brooding over for some time had now taken a strong hold on him. He was pretty sure it held the essential key to tracking down Isabel's harasser. But it was a theory he was reluctant to share with anyone else. Both Emma Hayes and Jack Cheney would immediately have their suspicions about his relationship with Isabel confirmed if he were to confide in them. He would have to operate solo for the time being, going against all the principles of police investigation and teamwork.

He was uncomfortably aware that both Emma Hayes and Jack Cheney, members of his team whom he viewed with high regard, were giving him a very wide berth this morning.

Jack came in now, moving as quietly as a cat to stand beside Max's desk. He gave one of his nervous hurrumphing coughs.

'Any joy, sir?' he asked, looking at the names scrolling down Max's screen.

'Joy is just about the last item on the agenda at the moment,' Max responded tersely.

'Sorry, sir. Still it's good we got The Batterer isn't it? I mean, we've a watertight case on him.'

'Yes Jack. I hope you didn't come in especially to tell me that.'

'Well, no sir. But we need to think about our successes don't we? Good for team morale.'

'Mmm.'

'If Isabel Bruce helps us to nail the hypodermic sender as well as The Batterer, she'll have killed two birds with one stone won't she, sir? Some lady!' The excited anticipation of the pursuit and capture of the criminal shone through in his voice.

Max turned slowly. His icy stare had the constable stepping backwards with alarm. 'I didn't quite catch that,' he told Jack, 'luckily for you. And please don't bother repeating it.'

'So what now, sir?' Jack asked uneasily.

'More door-to-door slogging around the area. Go on, Constable Cheney, what are you waiting for?'

With Jack despatched and Emma taking statements from further witnesses in the Gaunt case, Max felt free to pursue his own line of investigation.

He knew what he must do. He was convinced that the theory he had been forming was valid. He wished it were not so, because he knew that the train of events he was about to trigger could lead to his losing Isabel's love and trust forever. But he had no choice, he had to do it. Not for his reputation or the thrill of bringing a criminal to book, but for Isabel's safety and maybe her life.

He dialled Alastair Bruce's number in the Highlands.

'Mr Bruce, this is Inspector Max Hawthorne. I'm calling in an official capacity, sir. It would be very helpful if you could answer a few questions for me.'

Isabel phoned Esther and told her she had was not feeling at all well. She would be off sick for the next few days. It was something she had never done before – told lies in order to take time off work on the pretext of an illness she did not have. But, on the other hand, although she did not have the flu, she felt weak, exhausted and utterly defeated.

There was no way she could concentrate on business issues. All of her energy was directed at simply trying to live through the hours without sinking into a world of dark, terrifying fantasies about what this man who had fixed on her planned to do next. She was so frightened she felt as though there were a great hole in her chest.

She wanted Max to be there with. Holding her very close, never leaving her. But she knew he had to work, that only through his efforts would the fog of fear lift away from her.

She decided to keep busy. She polished every item of antique furniture in her flat, rubbing the mahogany table until it gleamed and she could see her white, strained face reflected in its surface. She put sheets and cotton shirts in the washer and when the tumbler had dried them, she ironed them with great care. She made herself endless cups of coffee and lived on biscuits and nibbles of cheese.

From time-to-time she lay curled on the sofa, going over her past, wondering if her torturer stalked there, somewhere in the shadows of her life. Maybe there was someone she had barely been aware of, even though he had been dangerously interested in her? But her memory refused to co-operate with her. Eventually she fell into a light sleep, worn out with her thoughts. Her dreams were fragmented and when she woke she couldn't get a grasp on them.

The time crawled, each new minute a potential threat.

Max called Emma Hayes into his office. He spoke very quietly as he told her what he had found out and what his next move was to be. He wanted Emma to come along with him on this difficult visit. He emphasise the need for tact and discretion – and great care.

At eight in the evening, Isabel received a call from Luisa's lover, Josh. He sounded anxious, distraught even.

'Isabel, the police have been to the flat. They've arrested Luisa. They've taken her off somewhere to help with their enquiries or whatever they call it.'

Isabel sank on to the chair beside the phone, trying to make sense of this astonishing new development. 'Where is she? Who arrested her?' she demanded, but already, somehow, she knew.

'I don't know,' Josh said. 'I wasn't there. I had to work late this evening. When I got in I found this note on the table. It simply said she'd been taken to the local station. Christ, Isabel, I'm frantic with worry. I don't know what to do.'

There was real emotion in his voice. 'Listen,' Isabel told him, 'I think I might be able to find something out about this. Give me a minute or so and I'll call you back.' Before he could ask any more questions, she swiftly dialled Max's station.

'Isabel Bruce,' she snapped to the woman answering the call. 'I need to speak to Inspector Hawthorne. Now!'

'He's engaged in one of the interview rooms, Miss Bruce. Is there anyone else you would like to speak to?'

'No. I'm the sister of Luisa Bruce. I've heard that she's been brought in to your station for questioning. Is that right?'

There was a brief pause. 'Yes, that is correct. Miss Bruce is here helping with enquiries.'

Isabel slammed down the phone and called Josh back. 'I've found out where she is, and I'm going round right away to sort it out.' Suddenly she was re-fuelled with energy.

'OK,' said Josh shakily. 'Should I come along too?' he wondered.

'No, let me do this on my own, I'll get back to you as soon as I've any news.'

She telephoned for a taxi, then swiftly tied her hair back and splashed cold water on her face. As the taxi drew up, she ran up the steps. The police officer from the car newly on watch outside the flat was already intercepting the taxi driver.

'It's all right,' Isabel told the officer. 'I phoned for this taxi. I'm going to the police station. Feel free to follow if you like.'

The officer began to voice a protest, but Isabel was already in the taxi. All sense of danger had left her – she was furious at the turn of events, that Max should go and seize her sisterl without explaining to her, Isabel, what he intended to do and why. Rage seethed within her. If the monster should turn up now, she felt she could strangle him with her bare hands with no difficulty at all.

At the station, she stormed in and banged on the counter of the reception area with her clenched fist. The officer on duty, who was frowning over paperwork, looked up and then hurried across.

'I'm Isabel Bruce. I'm currently under protection from some maniacal harasser.'

'Yes, madam, I'm aware of your case. What seems to be the problem?'

Isabel felt her eyes narrow but she made herself keep calm. 'I need to speak to Inspector Hawthorne. Something very...significant has just come up. Regarding my case. He needs to know about it.'

'I see. I believe Inspector Hawthorne is interviewing at present. I'll see if someone else on the team can speak to you.'

'No, I need to see the Inspector,' Isabel insisted. 'I can't speak about this matter to anyone else. I think you should tell him it's very urgent I see him right away.' Her eyes challenged the other woman not to make further objections.

The officer paused for a fraction of a second, then picked up an internal phone and punched in some numbers. Isabel listened as the woman recited the words she had just spoken, with admirable accuracy. 'He'll come along right away,' she said, replacing the phone. 'Perhaps you'd like to take a seat.' She gestured to the row of plastic chairs ranged along the wall, but Isabel had no intention of sitting quietly. She prowled the little waiting area like a tigress on the hunt.

Within seconds, Max appeared looking tired and strained. His dark hair was falling over his eyes and he pushed it back with a weary gesture.

Isabel swung round to face him and, for a moment, her anger against him dissolved. She realised with a sinking heart that she would never stop loving him. But that, after what had happened this evening, it would be surely impossible for them to reconcile their differences.

'We can't talk here,' he said quietly, leading the way down a dimly-lit corridor to a small office which had his name on the door printed on a small white plaque. He invited her to sit down and drew up a chair beside her.

'What the hell do you think you are doing arresting my sister?' Isabel demanded, her eyes blazing with fresh fury.

'She's helping with enquiries. She's not on a charge.'

'So why drag her here?'

'I didn't drag her. In fact it was at her request that I brought her here. She came quite readily. She said she would prefer to do that rather than have her boyfriend come home and find the police at her flat.'

Isabel thought about it. 'OK, I can understand that. But why is she here? Why?' she pleaded, not daring to even try to answer her own question.

'Because I have reason to believe she has some involvement in the harassment you've been subjected to.' He spoke in a low voice, meeting her gaze openly.

'No. *No!*' Dismay swept over her in a shuddering cold wave. 'You've made a terrible mistake. How could you think that of her, Max? She's my sister?'

'Yes. I'm sorry Isabel. I'm truly sorry.'

'You're sorry, is that all you can say? I can't believe what you're telling me. I won't believe it. The whole thing is utterly ridiculous.' Tell me this isn't happening, her eyes begged him. But her stomach was already churning with dreadful anxiety. She knew that Max would not act without good reason.

'Earlier today, I telephoned your father,' he told her.

'What?' Her body jerked as though an electric shock had been sent through it. 'How could you do that without consulting me first? He's an elderly, frail man and he's just come out of hospital.'

'I'm sorry Isabel. It was vital for me to speak to him for the furthering of the investigation.'

'Oh, don't feed me that police jargon,' she said impatiently. 'It still boils down to harassing a poor old man.'

'I didn't harass him,' Max said patiently. 'I simply gave him the option of answering some straightforward questions. And he was quite willing to oblige me.'

A worm of dread crawled within her as she braced

herself for what she was going to hear next. 'Go on,' she told Max dully.

'He told me that he had recently given your sister a substantial loan. He also mentioned that there had been many similar loans in the past but none of them had been repaid. He had told her that there would be no more money available.'

'I already knew that,' Isabel cut in dismissively.

'He also told her that he was in the process of altering his Will,' Max went on.

'Oh Heavens!' said Isabel in a strangled voice.

'He told Luisa that as she had had so much in the past, he had decided to cut her out of the financial bequests. He would be leaving her items of furniture and so on, but no money.'

Isabel stared at him, unable to speak.

'Apart from one or two modest bequests, the bulk of your father's money and the proceeds from his two substantial houses will go to you, Isabel.'

Isabel closed her eyes, trying to absorb this completely unexpected and shocking information. 'Dear God, she must hate me,' she whispered.

'She must have been upset when she heard, most certainly,' Max agreed.

'When did she hear?' Isabel's head jerked up and her tone was sharp.

'Whilst she was in Australia. There were one or two very acrimonious phone conversations between her and your father apparently.'

Isabel could imagine. 'Well then,' she said slowly, 'If Luisa was in Australia she couldn't have sent the letters. They were delivered by hand and she was on the other side of the world.'

'That's right.'

'So, it can't be her.' She looked at him in defiance and he looked thoughtful. She could tell he had an idea, some kind of working hypothesis of the truth behind this mess. But either he hadn't worked it out fully, or he was deliberately hiding it from her. For a wild second, she hated his cool, clinical arrogance. She wanted to strike him and made a livid red mark across his beautiful carved features.

'But the letter with the razor was delivered after her return,' Max pointed out.

'It came by post!'

'Yes. And Luisa was here in London to post it.'

'She didn't send that dreadful envelope. She didn't. I just know it. How can you even think such a thing, Max? She's my sister. She's part of my family. One of the only two members left.' She suddenly wanted to cry and had to fight the impulse with every fibre of her being.

'And anyway,' she went on desperately, 'even if Luisa hated me for being the one to get all Father's money, what would she have to gain by putting me through this terrible sadistic torture? It wouldn't make any difference to Father's Will. Besides which, she must surely know that when Father dies, I shall give her a fair share anyway.' Unless he ties it up so I can't, she thought worriedly, knowing her father's determination and ingenuity, not to mention that of his wily Scottish solicitor.

'Some form of revenge?' Max suggested. 'Anger and jealousy because your father favours you above her?'

'That's a dreadful thing to suggest. I can't even to bear to think about it!' she protested.

'It's something to work on,' he said quietly.

'Has she confessed to doing all these terrible things?'

'No, but neither has she denied any involvement.'

'What does that mean?'

'It means she's staying silent most of the time and when she speaks she's vague and evasive.'

'Has she got a solicitor with her?'

'Yes.'

'Are you holding her here?'

'Until the interview is finished, yes.'

'Can you do that?'

'Yes. We can hold her up to twenty-four hours. Then, unless we have sufficient evidence to charge her, we have to release her.'

She saw him once again as the dedicated, intense professional. Unbending, impersonal. Nothing mattered to him except upholding the law. Isabel stood up. 'There's no point our talking any further, Max. I want to see Luisa, talk things through with her. She'll tell me things she won't tell you.'

'No,' he said, 'I'm afraid you can't see her.'

'I insist,' Isabel flared at him. 'She's my sister and you can't stop me.'

'I can as a matter of fact,' he said evenly. 'But that isn't the issue. She's especially asked not to see you at present.'

'No, that can't be true!

'I wouldn't lie to you, Isabel.'

She looked at him. His eyes were hard but she believed him. She felt her world breaking up into pieces around her. Disbelief and anger and terror had all had a grip on her in the recent past. Now she simply felt a dazed, numbed kind of acceptance of what fate had thrown at her.

'Isabel,' he said, stepping close to her.

She sprang away from him. 'Don't! Don't touch me.'

She heard him swallow, saw a muscle twitching in his cheek. 'I'd like to take you home myself, darling,' he said, 'but I have to stay here.' He ran a hand through his hair. He looked wretched. 'I'm so sorry, so very sorry about all this. I hate it, the way things have turned out. Can't you see that?'

'Yes,' she said sadly. 'I know that's true. But we can't go on now, Max, can we? You've taken away my sister, stripped me of my trust for someone I've loved all my life. You've shown up my father as ruthless and vindictive. Maybe they were both flawed before, but if it hadn't been for your acuteness and tenacity, I'd never have known. How can I forget that? How can we have a future together after this?'

'Oh Isabel, my love.'

'It's over,' she said with soft finality. There was long, misery-filled silence.

'I still have a responsibility for your safety,' he told her, his lips tight.

'Then get Sergeant Hayes or Constable Cheney to take me home, please. Now.'

He hesitated, then swiftly left the room. Her legs trembled so violently she had to sit down again. Her life was in danger and her family was lost to her. She had rejected her lover because he had torn apart her world. The way ahead seemed nothing but darkness and misery.

chapter seventeen

In the morning, after a half-sleep filled with dreams where dark mysterious images waved like thick weeds in a slimy pond, Isabel dragged herself out of bed and took a long shower. She went into the kitchen and switched on the kettle. Outside in the garden, a bird sang with heart-breaking purity, as though the world was still a beautiful place.

She looked at her watch. Only seven-fifteen. What was she supposed to do with herself for the rest of the day? What point was there trying to do anything? What point was there to anything, full stop?

The phone pealed. Max! she thought, her heart racing in anticipation and then she remembered her violent rejection of him. Recalled the desolate set of his shoulders and that he had walked away from her the night before.

'Hello,' she said wearily.

'Isabel, it's Josh. I need to talk to you. I need to see you.'

'We talked last night, Josh. I haven't heard anything else yet.'

'No, but I've got something very important to tell you. We've got to meet.'

'Is it about Luisa?'

'Yes. We can help her. But I don't want to talk on the phone. The police might have tapped your line.'

'No, of course not.'

'How do you know?'

She thought about it. 'I suppose I don't. OK, where do you want to meet?'

'At the Pelican cafe near Tower Bridge. By St Katharine Docks. Do you know it?'

'I'll find it.'

She dressed in blue denim jeans and a black sweater. Flinging her cape around her, she ran out of the house and up the steps. The officer in the police car outside got out and came towards her. She noticed the children from across the road, watching solemnly. They must be getting some good entertainment from all this police surveillance, Isabel thought grimly. She felt relieved that Flo was still away visiting her sister.

'I'm taking a taxi to my hairdressers,' she informed the officer.

'I'll tail you Madam,' he said.

No, you won't, she said to herself, wanting to meet Josh without the interference of the police. She gave the officer the address of the salon in the High Street, then hailed a taxi at the end of the road. At her hairdressers, she made an appointment for the next week and then asked if she could use their cloakroom.

She had vaguely remembered that the window in the cloakroom was large enough to climb out of. With a sigh of mingled triumph and relief she managed to squeeze herself through. As she had expected she found herself in a little alleyway, from where she was able to walk back into the High Street, out of the view of the waiting police car. Dodging across the road, she hailed another taxi and told the driver to take her to the entry to St Katharine Docks.

Josh was waiting for her. He smiled as she walked up to him and she thought how attractive he was in a lightweight, boyish way. He put his arm around her protectively, ushered her into the cafe and ordered coffee and brioches for both of them.

'What is it you have to tell me?' she demanded urgently. 'Have you heard from Luisa?'

He shook his head. There was something about his eyes, so bright and alive, that puzzled Isabel. He should be looking more grave, weighed down with worry about Luisa.

He reached out and placed his hand over hers. 'It isn't Luisa I'm thinking about,' he said softly.

Isabel swallowed. Her throat felt tender and raw. 'What?'

'It's you I think of. You fill my mind. You're there all the time. And every night I see you walking in my dreams. I love you, Isabel,' he whispered. She could feel the intensity of his excitement tingling in the air around him.

There was a horrible sense of deja-vu, of sitting across the table from the charming Kelvin Gaunt and suddenly understanding the truth about him.

'It's you,' she whispered. 'You're the man who sent the letters and the hypodermic and the taxi for Highgate. You're the monster who's been ruining my life.'

'I'm not a monster, I'm mad about you.' he protested. 'They were love letters, don't you see?'

'Love letters,' she echoed, shaking her head. She recalled Max saying exactly that. Oh Max! If only you were here, I need you so much. 'What about Luisa?' she asked. 'What does she know about all this?'

'I'm not sure,' Josh said with a look of puzzled innocence. 'I suppose she'll have guessed quite a lot since the police took her, but not before. You were so considerate,

Isabel, weren't you? Whenever she mentioned that you looked pale or worried, you just brushed it aside. You didn't want to worry her by saying what was going on.' He smiled at her, fond and fired up with intense anticipation. 'You're so brave.'

Isabel felt her breath coming in rapid jerks as though she had been running. She made herself slow down, stretching out each breath. 'What do you want, Josh?' she asked trying to sound even and assured.

'You, of course,' he said, leaning close to her. 'Nobody can love you the way I love you, Isabel. The way I'll love you when we're alone together.'

'But we won't ever be together, Josh,' she said with gentle firmness, hoping he couldn't hear the thundering of her heart. 'I don't love you in that way.'

'No, you love Inspector Max Hawthorne,' Josh smiled. 'Oh, I know all about your secret love affair. I've been watching you. I know so much about you, Isabel.' His eyes glittered. 'And we will be together. Very soon.'

Isabel took a sip of coffee to moisten her dry mouth. Anxiety and fear buzzed in her head. Keep calm!

'It all started as a game,' Josh told her, his eyes darting busily over her face, fluttering and insect-like. 'Luisa phoned me from Australia to tell me that her father had cut her out of his will. She was so, so angry. She called him every name under the sun. She has a filthy tongue, doesn't she? And then she did a bit of bad-mouthing of you, the younger daughter Father loves best, the one who always did what he approved of, the one who worked hard and got all the goodies.'

'Does she hate me?' Isabel whispered.

'No, she loves you. She was just dead jealous. She wanted to hit back at you for having your father's approval and getting all his cash. So I offered to help. Give you a little aggro and grief. It was just a joke, a breeze.'

'A joke!' Isabel echoed, appalled. 'Sending a hypodermic, sending a razor blade. I had to go to hospital to be patched up.'

'I'm sorry.' He looked contrite, like a naughty little boy. 'I got carried away. I really regretted that.'

'But something like that is the product of a sick mind,' she protested. 'Are you sick Josh?'

'I'm just in love with you,' he said with a smile that chilled her bones. 'The razor wasn't my own idea, or the hypodermic. I was working on the set of a new thriller in the West End. It was about a stalker and I got the ideas from the script. And the necessary props too, incidentally.'

She put her head in her hands.

'I started watching the house. Following you around whenever I had time off work. I was very careful. Very clever. You never saw me did you?'

'No,' she said faintly.

'And then I fell in love with you.' He ran a finger down her cheek. His eyes glittered with a wild, crazy hunger. She blinked, willing herself not to recoil.

'What about the hair? The lock of my hair? How did you manage to get that?'

'Oh, that was easy!. I took it from Luisa's locket.'

Isabel had a sudden memory of a day years ago, of saying good-bye to Luisa before she went off on one of her working trips abroad. She hadn't wanted her big sister to go away. She had clung to her and Luisa had teasingly cut a slender lock of her hair and curled it into the Victorian locket that had belonged to their father's mother. 'I'll wear it all the time so a little part of you will be always be there with me, pet,' she had reassured the small, tearful Isabel.

'She doesn't wear the locket any more,' Josh said, watching the emotions on Isabel's face with intense interest. 'She likes those modern things made of wires and fake gems. She's rather tawdry isn't she?' he said, smiling and showing his shiny white teeth. 'By the side of you, I mean?'

Isabel stared at him, transfixed and speechless at this appalling new turn of events.

'And then there was the abortion,' Josh went on, making a grimace. 'I told her I didn't mind about it, but really I hated the whole business. Luisa has the morals of an alley cat, don't you think? She's an easy lay, a really modern woman. But you're so pure Isabel. I'll bet you've slept with no more than one or two men in your whole life.'

Isabel tried to clear the confusion swirling in her brain, the bewilderment of being shown the grotesque truth of the recent past. She knew she had to think of the future, of what to do next. How to get away from Josh…

'Where shall we go to make love, Isabel?' Josh asked, his big brown eyes sending little darts into hers. 'That's all I want. Just two or three hours when you're mine. After that I shall be off – I've got a flight booked, some friends in Spain to stay with, and a false passport. It's amazing what you can wangle if you just know the right people.'

'I can't make love with you,' Isabel whispered fiercely, panic suddenly overtaking her studied calm.

'Why not?'

'I'd be betraying Max.' Tears were banking up. She squeezed her eyelids together, knowing this was not the way to handle Josh. But the thought of giving herself to him was horrific. Almost worse than the prospect of pain and torture. 'I can give you money,' she said desperately. 'How much do you want?'

'I don't want money. I'm not interested in possessions. Except you – I want you, Isabel. I want to put my stamp on you forever. And it's going to happen. Because if not, I'm going to hurt Max in such a way that he'll never be able to make love to you again.'

Her mind sprang into red alert. She stared at Josh in dismay.

'Max is a very clever detective,' Josh said. 'It was a stroke of brilliance to guess at Luisa's involvement in this little project. But when he came for her yesterday, I guessed he'd soon realise she was just a link in the chain, a mainly-innocent bystander. I thought it would not be long before Max came back for me. So I cleared out of the flat and went to his place.'

'How did you know where he lived?'

'I followed him back from the police station one night. I'm very thorough when I get involved in a project.'

'What did you do then?' My God, he's an obsessive, she thought. He's disturbed. Crazy. What has he done to Max? Her heart felt as though it were being squeezed by iron fingers.

'I pressed all the entry bells on the security system outside his block of flats. And, of course, some obliging person activated the door release. It was simple then, I hid in an alcove close to the lift and just waited until he came back. As he put his key in the lock, I crept up and hit him with a baseball bat.'

'Oh no!'

'Don't worry. He was stunned and dazed, but only for a few moments. I opened the door and pushed him through. He fell on the floor and I tied his hands with garden wire. Then I bound his legs and it was easy after that. I poured him a whisky; he looked as though he needed it, poor guy. I added a couple of Luisa's sleeping pills and...well, I should imagine he'll have been pleasantly dreaming and will just be waking up around now.'

A sudden, still calm came over Isabel. She told herself to hold her emotions in check and to *think.* She willed her pulse to steady, her heart to beat normally. 'All right. Tell me exactly what you want me to do?' she said to Josh, bowing her head so he could not read her face.

'We'll go back to Max's flat and then you'll give me my two hours. Two hours to do whatever I like with you. Two hours to take you to that place where pain and ecstasy blend. You'll be quite safe, Isabel. Max will be there, watching and listening.'

'And if I refuse, you'll do what you like with Max instead?' she said dully. 'So I've no choice, have I?'

'No.'

'Very well, then. I agree.' She stood up and made a dramatic sweep across the table with her pashmina,, throwing it around her shoulder and drawing herself up like a stunning operatic Prima-Dona.

Josh imprisoned one of her hands, holding it in a claw-like grip as they walked along the pavements. He kept looking at her, smiling and smiling at the prospect of what he was going do to her. Isabel fixed her thoughts on Max; saving him was all she could carry in her mind, all that mattered.

The flat was in a small block on the North side of the Thames, around five minutes walk from Tower Bridge. Josh stretched out his free hand and pressed five buttons on the entry panel. Nothing happened. He pressed another five. The entry door gave a low buzzing sound and he pushed it open, pulling Isabel through. 'See! So much for security,' he said. 'Some people will open up no matter whose face they see on the video.'

They went up to the second floor in the lift. There seemed to be no one around. It was past nine now and people who had jobs would all have left the building. Josh held her hand tightly – his eyes feverish with excitement. He took a key from his pocket; presumably the one he had taken from Max the night before.

I've got one chance only, Isabel thought, steeling herself. As Josh turned the key and then pushed open the door with his foot, she brought her free arm up and poised herself to strike. But there was a sudden swift movement from inside, then arms flying in the air and a heavy muffled bang. Josh went sprawling on the floor. Isabel was grasping the pepper-pot she had swept from the table with her pashmina in the cafe. It was a plastic pot with a screw stopper at its base. She had managed to work the stopper free and had been ready to throw the pepper into Josh's face. Now, for a split second, she froze.

'Do it!' she heard Max hiss urgently. 'Now.'

As Josh struggled to get to his feet, she threw it in his face. He howled and threw his hands over his eyes. Vaguely, she registered Max slumped against the wall, his eyes dark holes in his face, his wrists red where the wire had cut him, his ankles cruelly bound with two, thick leather belts. White hot anger glowed in her like a poker. She needed to do real damage. She raised her foot and brought her high-heeled boot down on Josh's knee with all of her weight. There was a thud and he made a low groan. She raised her foot and brought it down once again in exactly the same place. This time he screamed. He clutched at her jeans but she shook him off.

She heard a voice calling, 'That's enough! Isabel. Stop. *Stop!*'

She looked down at Josh. He was whimpering. 'No more,' he begged. 'Please, I can't stand pain.'

Shaking and shocked, she stood quite still. Not taking her eyes from Josh, she took her mobile phone from its clip on her jeans and called the station. She heard words tumbling from her in a rush of panic. 'Isabel Bruce. We need help. Tell Sergeant Hayes. Now! At Max's flat. And Constable Cheney. Now! It's urgent.' Her lips were trembling, her throat seemed to have closed. She looked up at Max.

'You're doing fine,' he said in reassurance. 'They'll be here very soon.'

Josh was trying to turn himself, to crawl towards the door. His face was twisted with pain, his eyes red from the pepper she had thrown at him.

She lifted her leg. 'If you move one more inch, I'll start again.'

He fell back. 'No, Isabel, please. Oh, we could have had such a lovely time!' he moaned.

Max winced. 'Dear God!'

Isabel looked at her watch, looked at the door. 'Please come!' she prayed. She wanted to help Max, to cut the punishing wire from his wrists, but she dare not take her eyes from Josh for one second. She could feel Josh's evil crawling around in her skull like a living thing. Any minute, that evil might empower him and bring him back to full strength.

Then, suddenly, the door burst open and there was a blur of figures surging into the flat. Two uniformed police officers and Sergeant Hayes and Constable Cheney.

Max instantly took charge. 'We've got our suspect. One of you restrain him. Did you call an ambulance?'

'Yes sir,' Emma Hayes said.

'Get them to bring up a stretcher,' Max told Jack Cheney, indicating Josh's sprawled body.

'What about you, sir?' Emma asked. 'And Miss Bruce?'

'I'll need the help of some wire cutters, otherwise I'm fine.' He paused. 'Isabel must speak for herself but, just for the record, she's been heroic. Although I did wonder if we might have to put her on a charge for GBH!'

'It was self-defence,' Isabel protested. 'It was defence of you!'

She wanted to run to him and put her arms around him, to chide him for teasing her. To comfort him, to thank him for bringing a ray of light to this dreadful, brutal moment. Her own anger had amazed her. The energy and exhilaration and now, strangely, the remorse.

But once again, Max was Inspector Hawthorne, in command of his team. He was at work and she must keep a respectful distance.

Paramedics arrived with a stretcher and lifted Josh onto it.

'Go with him to the hospital,' Max told Jack Cheney. 'Take another officer with you. Keep him secure and don't let anyone else talk to him unless you're there – and caution him while you're on the way.'

'Right sir!' Jack sprang forward, his face alight with purpose.

Josh groaned as they manoeuvred him through the door. He turned and looked at Isabel. 'I love you,' he said with deep reproach.

While paramedics cut Max free of his restraints and bandaged his wrists, Emma made tea and then sat with Isabel in the tiny, pristine kitchen and questioned her about the morning's events.

'How is my sister?' Isabel asked when Emma laid down her notebook.

'She's been released. She's very shocked and upset, naturally.'

'Can I see her?'

'Oh yes. We're not going to press any charges against her.'

The two uniformed officers left. Emma went out into the corridor to make calls on her mobile.

Max and Emma held each other in trembling silence.

'You saved my life,' Max said simply. 'I truly believe he would have killed me if you hadn't played along with him and then found the courage to stop him in his tracks.'

'I've never laid a finger on anyone in my life before,' she said. 'The courage came from realising just how precious you are to me, Max. I'd have done anything just to make you safe.'

Swiftly Isabel filled him in on all that had happened since their bitter exchange the night before. From his final questioning of Luisa, Max had guessed at most of what she told him, although he had not known about Josh's work in the theatre or the way in which his knowledge of drama had fired his imagination and ingenuity during his harassment of Isabel.

By the time Emma came back, they found themselves exhausted with the events of the last few hours and were sitting very correctly apart, deep in their shared reflections.

Max looked up. 'Emma,' he said slowly, 'there's something I've been meaning to say to you and Jack about certain aspects of this case. It might be necessary for me leave the force. Isabel and I...'

'Please don't say any more, sir,' Emma interposed. 'Jack and I are both agreed that what we don't hear, we don't have anything untoward to report. We'd like to congratulate you for cracking this case, and, for the record we'd like you to know you're the best governor we've ever worked with. And now Miss Bruce's ordeal is over, I hope she'll soon feel better and be able to get on with her life in whatever way she wishes.'

She left and Max and Isabel looked at each other. He raised his eyebrows. 'She'll make Chief Constable in around ten years!'

And then they smiled the smile of two people who know exactly what is going on in the other's mind and heart. And after that he stood up and held out his arms to her.

chapter eighteen

Isabel and Max were married the following year in the little country church near Loch Melfort, where both Luisa and Isabel had been christened.

The months between Josh's arrest and the trial had been a strange, sometimes troubling, yet magical time for both of them. As Isabel was to appear in court as a key witness and Max was to give vital police evidence, they had had to keep their engagement very secret, and had only met in private. But after the trial and Josh's conviction, they were able to take up the life of a normal couple looking ahead with happiness to their marriage.

There was just one lingering worry that clouded Isabel's new found joy and that was her concern on Luisa's behalf. She had talked to Max at length about her feelings for her sister, how she longed to be reconciled with her, how Luisa's wretchedness and guilt about all that happened were keeping them apart.

'You have to give her time,' Max advised. 'Although she was only marginally implicated in what happened, she was very much in love with Josh to begin with, and became heavily influenced by him. Think how duped she must have felt, how humiliated when she found out what had been going on.'

'No matter how hard I try, I just don't seem to be able to get through to her,' Isabel told him sadly. 'We meet up, and we chat and have a drink together, but she's all enclosed within herself. Smiling, but brittle.'

'She's feeling guilty. It will take time for her to come to terms with what she got herself implicated in. Just keep plugging away,' he told Isabel gently, reflecting on the unfairness of life in making those who were sinned against feel almost as guilty as the sinners.

In his book, Luisa was the perfect actress, the consummate dissembler, both in her work and her private life. He recalled the evening he had arrived unannounced at her flat in order to question her on her possible involvement in the reign of terror to which Isabel was being subjected.

When she opened the door, her slightly-hooded eyes had registered curiosity, rather than alarm, at having a strange man ring her doorbell so late in the evening, at a time when many other women were thinking of retiring with a good book.

He remembered the languid sexiness of this elder half-sister of Isabel's, in complete contrast to the open candour of Isabel herself. How she had invited him into her flat and sat curled on her sofa, drawing languidly on a cigarette, watching him assessingly through the haze of smoke.

He had decided there was something sluttish, yet curiously appealing about her, and whilst she held no attraction for him personally, he guessed that she must have been a real man-eater in her youthful hey-day.

Her manner had been one of shrugging unconcern in response to his initial questions. When he had suggested she might have information that would help him to identify a man harassing a young woman in North London, she had simply smiled and told him she really didn't think she knew many stalkers.

But once he had told her the identity of the woman under threat, once he had mentioned Isabel's name, her sangfroid had instantly deserted her and he had judged that her dismay and shock were quite genuine.

Nevertheless, his overall assessment of her still remained that of a woman who was embittered, wilful, envious and greedy. But he had come to realise that there was a real and warm bond between the two half-sisters. He recognised that the quality of their love for each other was somewhat one-sided, the deepest and most unselfish emotions being those flowing from Isabel, but he felt it was important for their sisterly bond be preserved, if only for the sake of Isabel's happiness.

So when the wedding preparations got underway, and Isabel had been determined that Luisa should be her matron of honour, he had raised no objections, despite his private reservations.

'How are you going to engineer that, darling?' he had asked her tenderly. 'I should think Luisa herself might have some doubts about her rights to accept your generous invitation.' And astonishing forgiveness, he added to himself.

'Yes, I'm sure she will,' Isabel agreed, looking concerned.

She stared into Max's face. 'But what about you?' she wondered, a thought suddenly striking her. 'I've never asked you about your own feeling on this, have I Max? Oh darling, I'm sorry I didn't think to do that before, and I'd quite understand if you didn't want me to have Luisa as my matron of honour?' She gazed at him, her eyes clouded with this new anxiety. 'What do you say?'

'I want what you want, Isabel,' he said quietly. 'I know that's a horny old cliche, but it's the truth. If you really want this to happen at our wedding, then go ahead and make it happen.'

'I do.' She looked up at him her eyes brimming with love. 'Oh thank you for saying that Max!' she said, clasping her hands and looking so determined and earnest, he wanted to sweep her into his arms and make her forget all about her sister.

'I so want to make things right between me and Luisa,' she went on. 'And I really do want her to be there at the church, taking her rightful place as a member of the family. Apart from anything else, people who know me will think it very odd if I don't ask my own sister to be my attendant.'

'Well then, I suggest you take her out to lunch somewhere smart,' Max suggested with a wry smile. 'Feed her exquisite food and some beautiful wine, get her off her guard, then put your proposition to her. Maybe you'll have her eating out of your hand!'

Isabel leaned forward and kissed his lips. 'You're nothing short of brilliant, dearest husband-to-be! Maybe I'll do just that,' she said thoughtfully.

Soon afterwards she telephoned her sister and made an arrangement for them to meet and have lunch together in a little restaurant near Max's flat, close to Tower Bridge.

As usual, on answering the phone, Luisa sounded uneasy – a certain guardedness constantly edging into her voice.

'I've something very special to talk about with you,' Isabel told Luisa. 'We'll have a lovely lunch and a girlie chat, just like we used to years ago.'

Luisa was already waiting when Isabel arrived at the restaurant. This was unheard of! Luisa was notorious for being late for everyone and everything. Isabel realised instantly how anxious she must be.

When they hugged, Luisa pulled quickly away, prickly and uncertain.

'You look gorgeous,' Isabel told her as they settled to face each other across a table positioned by a vast picture window, looking out across the river traffic of the Thames. 'I love the new short haircut.'

'Time to move on,' Luisa said drily, inspecting the menu. 'Once you're hitting forty, long hair can begin to look ridiculous.'

They made their order and then there was an uncertain silence as they waited for their drinks to arrive.

'How's work?' Isabel asked, realising that she would have to make the running with the conversation. Luisa was clearly ill-at-ease and curiously at a loss. This was the first time they had dined out formally together since the terrifying day of Josh's arrrest.

'I've just landed a part in a new six-part TV drama. One of those sprawling saga things, taking a family through from the fifties to the present day. I'm playing a cameo part as the heroine's evil, grasping cousin.' She shot Isabel a sharp glance. 'Ironically appropriate, don't you think?'

'No, you're not evil,' Isabel told her softly.

Isabel forked up wild rocket and grated parmesan, then took a long sip of some very fine Vouvray. 'What's Max's opinion on that point?' she asked.

'That you started off something rather unpleasant when you were feeling at a low ebb and rejected by Father,' Isabel responded at last. 'And that, afterwards, you became inescapably involved in something quite different, something you had no possibility of guessing at.' That was more or less the truth, she thought, although she suspected Max had protected her from the tougher aspects of his appraisal of her sister.

'In other words I was both wicked and blind?' Luisa commented in dry, sceptical tones.

'No!'

'I rather think so!' Luisa said firmly. 'Oh, Izzie, darling, you're such a love to try to see me in such a good light. And a hundred-thousand times better a person than I'll ever be,' she added sadly. 'And for the record, that Max of yours is dauntingly impressive all round as well. Intelligent, sensitive, gorgeous-looking and impossible sexy. I think he almost deserves you.'

She raised her glass to Isabel in a gesture of toasting her happiness, and her blue eyes sparkled. 'So, tell me, how are the grand nuptial preparations going?'

'Very well,' Isabel said. She took a long drink of her wine, then placed the glass carefully on the table and took a deep breath. 'I want you to be my matron of honour, Luisa.'

Luisa stared at her, then gave a disbelieving laugh. 'What did you say? Did I hear you properly?'

'Yes.' Isabel waited.

Luisa fiddled with her almost-empty glass. The sunlight from the window caught the pale golden liquid resting at the base of the glass and sent tiny needles of gilded radiance onto the table. 'No, I can't,' Luisa told her. 'For one thing, I'm too old and raddled. But most important, I don't deserve to be asked,' she concluded sadly.

'What happened with Josh was not your fault,' Isabel told her. 'You've got to learn to forgive yourself.'

'No,' Luisa protested, 'I can't rid myself of responsibility all that easily. I was the one who started it all, and I did it because I was so jealous of you, and I made the mistake of moaning about it to Josh. I just never dreamed...'

'You're my only sister – and I love you,' Isabel broke in, stoically determined not to lose this particular battle. 'So will you please shut up and stop whinging. And it's not as if I'm asking you to wear a dress like a pink frothy meringue. You can wear black satin slit up to the thigh if you want.'

Luisa took a deep draught of her Vouvray, held it in her mouth for a moment, then swallowed. She looked directly into her sister's eyes. 'You're amazing Isabel. I can't believe anyone could be so generously forgiving as you are being to me. But, of course, you're as stubborn as an ox when you get an idea into your head. You take after our dear Father in that respect.'

Isabel smiled. 'So?'

'So, I don't see any point going on arguing with you. And thank you so much for asking, darling.' She laid her hand over Isabel's, and suddenly she smiled. 'But I'm not into black for weddings. And I'm sure your lovely Max would be most disapproving of my appearing at your marriage looking like a siren, and I would be decidedly wary about rousing his displeasure. He can be quite scary. So how about lilac?'

'Lilac, it is!' Isabel smiled.

'She's agreed,' Isabel told Max over supper that evening. 'Lunch did the trick, and cost me a fortune.'

'Only the best for Luisa,' Max commented dryly.

'I know. I'm not blind to her faults, even though I love her.' She hesitated. 'There's just one problem.'

Max narrowed his eyes in thought. 'Your Father won't have her darkening his doorstep, let alone the altar rails – is that it?'

'Yes.'

'You do understand that I never told him anything about

the true danger you were in, or of Luisa's involvement? I merely told him I needed information to help rule her out of our enquiries.'

'Yes, of course I know that. And Father has no idea of her link with Josh. Her latest abortion and her debts were quite enough to make him snap.'

'Do you want me to go up to Scotland and talk to him?' he asked gently. 'Turn on the full heat of my diplomatic skills?'

'Yes!' She sighed in relief. 'Oh Max, you're so good to me. Yes, yes, yes!'

'OK. It's a deal.' He stood up and came to stand very close to her, running a finger down her cheek. 'But I shall demand my payment in advance,' he whispered, slipping his hand inside her blouse and circling her breast with a feather-light caress. 'So shall we stop talking about your sister and get down to some serious male-female bonding?'

For the wedding, both the bride and matron of honour wore classic sheath dresses in heavy silk. Isabel was in ivory and Luisa in delicate fuchsia lilac.

'The beautiful Bruce sisters,' Mrs Pringle murmured fondly when she saw them coming up the aisle, Isabel luminous and radiant holding her father's arm. 'And the family all united again.' The joy of it brought tears to her eyes, which she quickly dabbed away with a snowy lace handkerchief.

Shortly before the wedding, Mrs Pringle had confided to Isabel that there had been a real scare for her father at the time he went into hospital. He had not gone in for tests on his heart at all but to have a suspiciously angry-looking mole on his leg removed. The operation had been simple and successful and no malignancy had been found.

'He was so worried before he had the surgery. But he wouldn't let me breathe a word to anyone, the stubborn man,' Mrs Pringle said. 'I hated to keep it from you, my dear. And from Luisa too,' she added hastily. 'But what can you do when your Father isssues an order?'

'Obey,' said Isabel, laughing and giving Mrs Pringle a hug.

'Now, tell me dearie, what do you think about Luisa's new gentleman friend?' Mrs Pringle had enquired, her eyes glinting with speculation.

Luisa had surprised them all at the last minute by bringing along Hector McFarlane as her special guest to the wedding. Hector was an old family friend, a widower of around fifty. He was cuddly and bald, immensely rich, had nothing whatsoever to do with the theatre, and gazed at Luisa as though she had been fashioned from diamond-encrusted egg shells.

'Perfect,' Isabel said. 'And even Father heartily approves.'

'Perfect,' she murmured again to Max as they stood outside the church as man and wife, and she looked lovingly at him, stern-faced and slightly uneasy in his grey tail-coat and pin-striped trousers as he faced the cameras.

She took his hand and squeezed it tightly. 'I love you so much, it almost scares me.'

He smiled. 'No need to be frightened. I'll be here beside you for ever.' He bent his head towards her.

Luisa grinned, grabbed Hector's camcorder and pointed it at the newly-weds as Max took Isabel in his arms and kissed her with his characteristic thoroughness.

Romance at its best from Heartline Books™

We're sure that you've enjoyed the latest selection of titles from Heartline. We can offer you even more new novels by our talented authors over the coming months. Heartline will be bringing you stories with a dash of mystery, some which are tinged with humour and others highlighting the passion and pain of love lost and re-discovered. Our unique and eye-catching covers will capture backdrops which include the glamorous, exotic desert, an idyllic watermill in the English countryside and the charm of a traditional bookshop.

Whatever the setting, you can be sure that our heroes and heroines will be people you will care about and want to spend time with. Authors we shall be featuring will include Angela Drake, Harriet Wilson and Clare Tyler, while each month we will do our best to bring you an author making her sparkling debut in the world of romantic fiction.

If you've enjoyed these books why not tell all your friends and relatives that they, too, can start a new romance with Heartline Books today, by applying for their own, **ABSOLUTELY FREE**, copy of Natalie Fox's LOVE IS FOREVER. To obtain their free book, they can:

- visit our website: www.heartlinebooks.com
- *or* telephone the Heartline Hotline on 0845 6000504
- *or* enter their details on the form below, tear it off and send it to: Heartline Books,
  FREEPOST LON 16243, Swindon, SN2 8LA

And, like you, they can discover the joys of subscribing to Heartline Books, including:

♥ A wide range of quality romantic fiction delivered to their door each month

♥ A monthly newsletter packed with special offers, competitions, celebrity interviews and other exciting features

♥ A bright, fresh, new website created just for our readers

Please send me my free copy of *Love is Forever*:

Name (IN BLOCK CAPITALS)

____

Address (IN BLOCK CAPITALS)

____

____

____

____________________ Postcode ______________

If you do not wish to receive selected offers from other companies, please tick the box ☐

If we do not hear from you within the next ten days, we will be sending you four exciting new romantic novels at a price of £3.99 each, plus £1 p&p. Thereafter, each time you buy our books, we will send you a further pack of four titles.